FROM THE AUTHOR

Fiction 4-Pack #2 is a four story collection of my works. In addition to the titles on the cover, there is a story about a special dog - it appears here for the first time and this will be its only publishing.

Hope you enjoy,
Chris

CHRISTOPHER WATSON

4FICTION -PACK #2

ELSEWHERE

E P
PUBLISHING

Fiction 4-Pack #2

Published 2013 by Elsewhere Publishing
www.elsewherepublishing.com

ISBN-13: 978-1-62538-030-2

Elsewhere Publishing
www.elsewherepublishing.com

Contents:

Extras:

Dedicated to:
family and friends
mentors and minions
Kay McGarvey

CHRISTOPHER WATSON

4FICTION
-PACK #1

The Jeweler's Daughter

Las Vegas. Home to more lost souls per capita than any other city -- making it the brightest beacon on the material plane to Outsiders. Outsiders who want to come in…

John Black earns his living by pretending to be a priest so he gets the call to boot these uninvited guests.

No demon possession is standard, but something about this one prompts John into lowering his guard. Will he survive?

ONE

"LIAR!"

Reverend John Black's satchel flew from his grip as he reeled backward. He stumbled to recover his balance. Each rapid clack of his dress shoes on the concrete moved him closer to the steep beveled steps he had admired upon arrival. Nearly caught up to the force of the shove, John spun to estimate where his broken teeth would end up if he face-planted.

He kicked a leg out and used a sliding stop he learned while being taught how to skate. His heel left a long black mark on the concrete, matching the contrails in the noonday Las Vegas sky.

"Look." John straightened his frock and pivoted. "Unlike demons, I'm not going to stay where I'm not wanted. But before I go, I need to verify." He patted his pockets before producing a Post-It pad with the potential client's name. "This is where Beverly Schmidt lives, right?"

The doorman's massive arms–rivaling some of the lesser demons John occasionally played poker with–

unfolded to reveal a black cross with a red censor circle on a worn t-shirt. Knuckle pops drew John's attention to meaty, balled fists. His voice, a low and dangerous whisper. "Get off my property, charlatan."

"Alright." John shrugged and mumbled loudly while he retrieved his satchel. "This is why I started charging a *call fee*." He nodded to the scowling man and summoned a pleasant smile. "Right. Good luck with the possession."

The man jabbed his thumb into his faded shirt. "See this?"

John paused to look at the faded logo. "Yeah."

"Know what it means?"

"I guess." John's eyebrows rose and lips parted. He recalled the matching bumper stickers on the new his-and-her Dodge Chargers in the driveway. The infernal engine he had under the hood of his classic '78 Charger would waste both of them. His mouth closed for a moment as he edited the snark from his reply for a deadpan delivery. "You like the band Bad Religion."

"No." The guys eyes flicked down to the logo. "Well, yeah, but I also wear it because I don't believe in God."

John *hmph*ed and eyed the band's logo. Four sharp replies raced through his brain, each jockeying for lead position. He pressed his lips tight. "Just to be clear–" John paused before he guessed, "Mister Schmidt?"

Set not to agree with anything, the man gave a slight nod.

"This is about demons, not God."

A soft burst of pungent sulfuric air rolled from the house. Profane power crawled along John's skin.

As though called to attention, his arm hair stood on end from goose bumps. In he yard, grass waved and saplings swayed.

He faced Schmidt to ask about it.

Schmidt's eyes widened and he shook his head slightly to say *No* to whatever John's question would have been.

"And not believing in demons, when one is in a loved one, is like hoping ignorance of gravity will keep you from falling after walking off a cliff."

Schmidt's eyes narrowed.

John moved from cartoon physics to the reality the muscled man tried to pretend not to notice. "Those puffs of air are not as pungent as they used to be, right?"

Schmidt continued to stare.

"But a general unease has been growing with each passing–" John slid his sleeve back as though to check a watch, but studied how straight the hairs were to estimate the length of the possession. "–day. That's because *whatever* is in your *whoever* is getting stronger."

John knelt, lowered his satchel, and rummaged through his bag of symbols. Given Mister Schmidt's dislike of Christianity, he moved his hand past the various crosses and pulled out a stick he had found camping. It did not have any powers but was fairly straight, pointy, and looked very much like a wand.

He pointed the stick beyond Mister Schmidt.

Cautious, the bodybuilder leaned to the side as to make sure he was not in the line of fire for whatever it was the stick did. A common reaction. No one ever stood their ground.

"Look." John kept eye contact with Mister Schmidt as he dipped his hand back in the bag, fishing. His fingers slid past the cool iron crosses and coarse pinecones to find the pommel of his House Palustuk dagger next to the canteen of holy water. The rough demonhide on the grip unraveled from the weapon and wrapped around his hand. Like a shoe tied painfully tight, the weapon bonded. "You said you don't believe in God, so I'm going to square with you."

Mister Schmidt took a small step back. "Okay…"

John shrugged. "Neither do I. However–" He pulled the dagger from the satchel. As though highlighted, the sulfur in the air glittered gold before being sucked into the knife. "People tend to be more trusting of a person with a large silver knife against a loved one's throat when they believe that person is of the cloth."

Schmidt's jaw slowly parted as his gaze wandered the curves and points of the ornate and deadly design.

"Now, if I leave, another person will eventually come." To grant a better view, John rotated the weapon to show the length. "This person–who will be very religious–will help you for free. Their main goal will be getting rid of the demon."

John slid the satchel's long strap over his shoulder and stood. "But when they are done, if your loved one survives, they will be horribly scarred."

Schmidt closed his mouth and gulped.

"Demon slaying is a real nasty business." John heaved a relaxing sigh. He had never been completely honest with a client and found it refreshing. Perhaps he'd finally be able to skip the post-job guilt. "I am not a slayer."

"You're not?"

"No." John shook his head. "Hell, I'm not even a Reverend."

Mister Schmidt's stare broke from the dagger and became distrustful again. "Then why–"

"I tried billing myself as a demon slayer once." John tucked the stick into the open satchel. "But look at me."

Schmidt's eyes scanned John's narrow frame.

"People expect a demon slayer to be over six feet tall, rugged, and mountainous." John motioned from his brow downward. "I'm skinny, can't grow a beard to save my life, and the only way I get close to six feet is on my tiptoes."

"Then why not call yourself an exorcist?"

"Because people expect them to be wizened elders with an air of understanding that'll be able to make the most defiant bend a knee with only a glance." John motioned to his head. "Having just turned thirty, it'd be impossible for me to pull any of that off…" He gave a smile.

Schmidt smiled back.

"Plus, I kind of got a friendly face."

Schmidt nodded. "If you're not a reverend, a demon slayer or an exorcist, then what are you?"

"I'm a demon *inconveniencer*."

"A what?"

John looked around the neighborhood. Like smaller housing communities in the suburbs of Las Vegas' urban sprawl, these manses were structured off the same four or five floor plans. Also, like the suburbs, shutters parted for neighbors to peer at the priest with a large silver dagger. "Can we take this inside?"

Schmidt hesitated, then nodded and backed into his house.

Mentally preparing for the heat always present from nether creatures breaching the material plane, John took a moment. In that moment, he crossed himself and gave an apologetic look to Mister Schmidt. "Only for appearances."

"Shit, it'll be the focus of the next homeowners association meeting." Schmidt gave a sly smile. "Do it again."

John chuckled.

Quickly approaching pats, like a cerebus pup, came from the driveway behind him.

He spun to brandish the blade.

A svelte body, like one of Lou's cocktail servers, stood in a pink running outfit. The gun she aimed at him held his attention.

Ready to take control of his body to potentially deflect the bullet, the demonhide tightened further.

John's hand became white and red where the blackened leather did not wrap. He kept control and refused to grimace.

Her teeth, in the muzzle's background, moved. "Do it and die, creep."

"Honey," Mister Schmidt cooed, "this is *Reverend* Black."

She glanced over John's shoulder and trained her pistol at the ground.

He lowered the blade.

The hide wrap loosened to allow blood flow.

John gave a sheepish grin. "Just responding to your call." He kept his eyes from wandering below her glistening, ripped shoulders. With a respectful slight bow, he apologized, "Sorry about that, Beverly."

"Laura," the woman corrected. She slipped her gun into a secret pocket behind her fanny pack.

John kept his eyes from straying as she moved past, trailing a faint flowery scent.

She took Mister Schmidt's extended hand and stood inside the entry. "Beverly is our daughter."

John felt his brow tighten as his gaze dropped to the concrete. Had anyone ever called in their own possession before?

Over the course of the last nine years, Lou, his boss, had regaled John with some of the more wild tales from the inconveniencers before him. Tales of Katzkyk, an imp who regularly breeched the mortal realm, were his favorite. The wily little guy had done some amazing things to hide his presence and extend his stay, but none of Katzkyk's crazy tactics involved telling on himself.

"Reverend." Laura pulled her husband further into the darkened house. "Please, do come in."

The tightness between his shoulder blades pulled on John's muscles. He hated jobs like this. Lou had told him cautionary tales of demons laying traps for real demon slayers, exorcists, and reverends.

With his dagger slightly extended, John drew a breath, crossed himself again, and entered.

Two

His arm hairs fully relaxed. John checked his watch. It took four minutes; the demon would only need four more days to complete its domination of the host's will. Their house did not reek of sulfur anymore. He nodded. After the first couple of days, the hourly pulses caused by the breech contained less brimstone as the rift leaked air from the mortal realm into the beyond.

John always imagined demons crowded around the rift on their side, sniffing the fresh air like depraved junkies. "Your wife's right, Mike," John corrected Mister Schmidt who, in trying to make the name sound feminine, added emphasis to the vowels. "The name's pronounced Mitzolkzka. It's a male demon."

Mike's face paled. He dropped his water bottle.

Laura caught it. "Demons have gender?"

The smell of her apple crisp recovery bar began to sink in. John regretted not accepting her earlier offer to have one. "Yes. Three actually. Male, female, and one-" He paused to rock his hand and spoke through a grimace, "That's sort of both."

Mike plopped on a loveseat.

Only able to steal a glance when Mike took the mini-sofa from their horrible zebra-striped den, John admired the room full of large beanbags. He wanted one, but could never justify the cost.

Laura sipped from the bottle, then asked, "What about angels?"

"Don't know," John shrugged. He eyed the tight spiral marble staircase and the silver-railed walkways it sprouted, leading to the second and third floor. Their entryway mirrored the kind of Greek decor found in the Forum Shops at Caesar's Palace.

Mike still looked out of it.

"Never seen one." Given how well she'd taken everything, and how she aimed her gun at him, she was a cop or similar. He decided to risk the truth with her, too. "Frankly, I'm not sure they even exist."

Her eyes widened and her mouth worked, but no questions came.

John bit his lip. Laura's reaction told him what he had missed. Mike was a skeptic; she believed.

To keep from making eye contact, he looked at the black and white striped walls. He tried to make it sound as though he were completing his thought. "On the material realm."

Laura's eyes lowered, searching for a way to ask what all believers eventually asked him.

Metaphysical conversations were the worst.

To direct the conversation away from where it would eventually end, John requested, "If I may ask, why didn't you guys reach out to someone before now?"

Both were lost in thought.

Guilt usually shook clients from their quiet reserve. These two needed something more. He cleared his throat. "How could you learn the demon's name and remain clueless to the fact that your daughter was possessed?"

"I," Mike began, then pointed to luggage hastily dropped down a hallway nearly as long as John's walk from the elevator to his condo. He continued, "We just returned from an overseas trip. I," Mike took Laura's hand "We, sort of heard it after the first pulse."

"Yeah, it was unnatural." Laura shook her head. "My adrenaline surged and I had an overwhelming urge to run." She frowned. "Not *go for a run*, just *run!*" Shame weighed on her eyelids, and she quieted. "So I did."

"Best reaction to have." John congratulated her and pulled the pointy stick again. "Striking terror in the bold helps isolate what kind of demon we're working with here." Hoping for more clues, he waved the stick at the stairs to buy more time and nodded as though he unearthed information beyond their grasp.

Mike had returned to looking at his feet.

John poked the massive shoulder with the stick to keep him from shutting down. "It's those that don't run that tend to get eaten."

"I'm not the curious type, but–" Mike rubbed where John jabbed. "A curiosity unlike anything I have ever felt took a hold of me." He cast his eyes upward as though he could look to the third floor. "I had to go see."

Focused on reading Mike, John leaned in. "What did you see?"

"I–" Mike shuddered. He worked his shoulders as though he were trying to remove a vest that would not come loose. He went still, and his gaze dropped. "I don't remember."

Curiosity in a non-believer was quite common, but what kind of demon could make skeptics uncomfortable with the truth and force them to shut out a memory?

A threatening, profane pulse rolled through the house.

Laura bolted out the door.

"No!" Eyes wide at John, Mike shook his head, "I don't want to see!" An infernal spark flashed in his eyes. "I don't want to serve!"

John hid the dagger behind his back.

Mister Schmidt's eyes became wreathed with flames.

John nodded. Demons often piggybacked on one another's senses. Just as humans tried to humanize demons, demons often believe humans capable of doing the same things their kind could. "Hi, Bev." John smiled, leaned in, and waved. "It's your Uncle John. Just came from Providence and brought you a gift."

Mike's mouth opened and worked the air as though his lips could lock onto syllables to express his thoughts.

A demon who could observe, but not control? Weird.

"Sorry, honey. Your projection isn't working." John winked. "Don't worry, though. I'll be up shortly with your gift." He took a step backward toward the stairs. "See you at the top."

The fire went out.

Mike rubbed his eyes furiously. "Ow."

"Easy, Mister Schmidt." John tucked the stick under his arm to place his hand over Mike's and kept him from further agitating his eyes. "It's only mental. Your eyes aren't on fire. Do you feel any heat? You're fine."

Schmidt took sips of air. "What was that?"

"Mitzolkzka knows I'm here."

"How?"

"Once in possession, demons instantly set markers to claim their territory. He felt me, a person not of direct relation to his vessel–" John paused too late to stop the word. "Not directly related to your daughter. He tried being patient. But since I didn't leave on my own, he flexed his profane might to make me act on instinct."

Mike bobbed his head. "What did you do?"

"I said *hi*."

"What?" Mike grabbed at John's hand like a drowning man. "How did you resist?"

"Different jobs have different requirements." Memory of the pulse Szalkyk had emitted after he swept the demon's remaining chips the night before elicited a proud grin. "My default is to not lose my shit when a demon flexes their otherworldly might." John considered the feeling. "It actually brings me into focus."

"What else is there to being an inconveniencer?"

John blinked at the question.

Of the many queries over the years, this one set him aback. Just the other night, Lou stated he should start training others. "Well, it's not that hard of a job, really." He pulled slightly.

Mike let go.

"When a demon first comes over, they are not used to our dim, chilly, smoke-free environment. So, many of them usually manifest by striking out at those around them, speaking in tongues, and generally making asses of themselves." John shrugged. "The amount of wit you need to trick them into returning is the equivalent of Bugs getting Daffy to say *duck season*."

Mike's studious facial expression didn't change.

"Get it?"

Mike shook his head.

Disappointment turned John's lips. It was funny to him. Strike one. He stepped back, pulled his stick, and pointed to the top of the stairs. "Being able to possess a sentient body already acclimated to our plane makes their transition easier." He raised his eyebrows to hint at the job title. "One might even say *our bodies* are rather *convenient* for them."

Schmidt's look remained wanting.

"Once they establish some sort of dominance, talking or tricking them out becomes more difficult, but there are–"

"Force?" Mike pounded his fist into his palm. "Can't you just use force?

Strike two. "Only if you want what damage they've wreaked to remain." John sighed as he abandoned the earlier explanation. "If they choose to leave, nearly all the wrong they've done is undone."

Mike offered, "Faith?"

John heaved another sigh. Strike three.

"Magic, then?"

"Look." John ignored the last desperate guess. "I'm heading up. It's imperative that I not be interrupted."

Dejected, Mike's gaze went back to his feet. "Okay."

John hiked his satchel strap higher on his shoulder and faced the stairs.

The grey-veined white marble radiated off-white power like the headlights that stayed on after the car was turned off. The air around the stairs turned to Jell-o and smelled of cotton candy.

Though he used to enjoy both gelatin and the spun confection, due to their prevalence during possessions, he'd learn to loathe them.

John pressed his shoulders through the thickened air. Though stale and still, the resistance was like walking through a wind tunnel.

Closer to the stairs, the slick sheen stood out like an old, rotted Pinto at an exotic car show. He grimaced and looked for an elevator. These folks were wealthy and eccentric enough to possibly have one.

That last thing he wanted was to make it to the top and be pushed backward by a waiting Mitzolkzka. It'd be an exceptionally long trip down tightly spiraled, slick marble stairs with a very sharp knife and a pointy stick.

Not finding one, John began his slog up the treacher-ous staircase.

THREE

THE VEINS ON JOHN'S TEMPLES PULSED HARDER AS HE made the fourth turn. One more blood-pumping, sweat-oozing round up the tight spiral and he would be on the third floor.

Uprooting devils who've established a foothold always proved to be challenging, but Mitzolkzka's aura made the stairs feel like hiking up a sand dune in Death Valley during the height of a brutal California heat wave.

He ascended, but the climb felt as though he were fighting to descend on an upside-down staircase with a weighted yoke.

The stairs began to ripple and turn.

Before the vertigo worsened, he drew a breath, narrowed his eyes against the thumping in his skull, and stroked his clerical collar.

Power radiated from the investment, eliciting a faint, otherworldly growl from his throat. A ringing filled his ears before his nose and mouth filled with voluminous sulfuric fumes.

John coughed smoke until the thick plumes became faint wisps.

The infernal warding restored his equilibrium, cooled the air, and beat away the other physiological obstacles.

He glanced at the back of his wrist. The case over his Rolex, the only inheritance from his father, opened like a peel bug. Flaming numbers marked five minutes, then began to count down.

Mouth caked with bitter ash, he focused on not swallowing the tainted residue. Last time he did, his stool shot from him for a week in painful splats like forced ketchup packets full of tar. Worse, his bowel movements reeked like a broken sewer main.

John took the remaining stairs in four hefts. He dropped the stick and pulled out a round apple juice bottle filled with holy water and took a sip.

Swishing it around in his mouth, the ashen batter cleared.

He regularly imagined, and hoped, the water would have a flavor or a wintergreen, lung-opening effect. But, yet again, it was simply water. Swishing it around, the crust in his nostrils cracked and soot fell from his nose.

John spat back into the bottle and watched the ebon-streaked fluid turn clear.

He nodded, screwed the top back on, and strapped it back in his satchel. Leaving the stick where he set it, he pulled the sheet with Beverly's name on it from the small Post-It pad. John palmed the name, gripped the knife, and proceeded to the bedroom door.

The UNLV-plastered entry reminded him of his failed attempt at becoming a history teacher. No one would confirm it, but John figured he was the quickest to be placed on academic probation and released by the college.

The door flew open.

He gritted his teeth, brandished the knife, and braced for the coming charge.

Instead of facing a demon's wrath, he was presented with the back of a young lady in a long nightshirt. Ignoring her body, John searched for an anchor.

Her wrist and ankles where free.

Her neck and crown were clear.

Her hands and feet were not bound.

John scanned the six focal points of possession again with the same results. "What the heck?" She was unfettered. Her flesh even lacked the faint glow of dominion. He cleared his throat. "Beverly?"

"No!" Thunderous growls echoed her alto voice. Her skin flushed. The nightshirt billowed. Her physical body did not change, but the cloth lifted and filled to take on the shape of a demon's powerfully built back.

Against conscious thought, John's eyes flicked to her backside, slightly revealed.

A compact disc shot from under the bed and whizzed by his head.

The door slammed shut.

John glanced at a newly formed disc slit in the drywall. Just like that, it could have been over. He scolded his wandering eyes, "Keep your head in the game."

He eased to the door and wedged as much of his body as he could in the corner next to the doorjamb. "Beverly, I have a gift for you."

Only the demonic booms came through the door. "She doesn't want it."

"Then for you, Mitzolkzka."

"I don't want it either."

"Aw, come on Mitzy-baby. Don't be like that," John cooed. "Tell you what. Just take a little look. If neither of you want it, I'll leave." He paused to let the token play.

The door remained closed.

Switching to a tactic that had yet to fail, John continued, "Better yet, Mitzolkzka, if you consider this gift, this tribute, I promise–God as my witness– that me and her parents will leave you alone until you figure out whatever is going on."

John gave his lips a nervous lick. Would this be the first demon in possession to refuse the bait of being left alone?

A soft click signaled the door unlatching, and warmth poured from the slightly opened door.

"Okay sweetie, check this memento out." He eased the large knife into view.

"Shit." The demonic base fled her voice.

To present all sides, John rolled his wrist and rotated the blade.

The echo faded as Mitzolkzka ended a string of profane curses with, "Shit. Shit."

John smiled. "I take that to mean you know what this is, then?"

"Yeah." Her tone took on the sound of a bashful child who had gotten caught doing something she shouldn't have.

He kept his amusement under wraps. "So, I take it that you are going to be civil?"

"What choice do I have?"

"None, really." John gave the blade another rotation. "May I enter, Mitzy?"

"Yeah."

The marker-stricken academic calendar moved away from him as the door creaked open. Keeping the knife in front of him, John eased his way into the room.

Four

THE NIGHTSHIRT FELL AGAINST BEVERLY'S BODY AS Mitzolkzka walked her to a chair. It was a lumbering, male demon walk.

John did not ogle the lithe body beneath the oversized shirt. He'd crossed into the demon's danger zone. The stakes were raised.

No matter what kind of afterlife there was, John didn't want *perversion* to be his cause of death. Lou would know. His boss would share it with the demonic poker players, and they all would have a hellacious round of laughter at his ultimate expense.

"Listen." John waved his hand by his nose as though he could bat away the cotton candy stink. "I'd prefer brimstone."

"Oh."

As the smell dissipated, John wondered what about demonic possession made the area smell of the spun confection. He wanted to ask, didn't want to risk the script. "You know there are ways to comfortably breech."

Coy, Mitzolkzka oscillated on her swivel chair. "Yeah."

Either not knowing, or not caring, the demon sat with her knees parted. John moved to the opposite side of the California king bed so the mound of shredded pillows–piled like a chopped salad–kept Beverly's lower body from view.

"I don't recall the symbol of House Palztonk being so-" Mitzolka waved her hand toward the knife. "So big."

Keeping the paper palmed, John fetched the authentic toothpick-length plastic cocktail stirrer from his inner pocket. "Don't doubt or fret, Mitzy." John presented the bona fide emblem gifted to him by Lou after his first inconveniencing. "I'm legit."

"Okay." Passive, Mitzolkzka fixed her brown eyes on him with a relaxed, cat-like disinterest. He crossed her legs. "What now, Representative?"

The hair on the back of John's neck went on end. He kept suspicion from narrowing his eyes.

"Isn't this where you're supposed to tell me about the four safe houses?"

About to answer, John paused. This guy spoke like a pro. He had the knowledge of a habitual breecher, but none of the wisdom.

"And how I'm supposed to broker passage through Izalk, Kroztk, Palztonk, or Wzok." He raised a finger, then pointed. "I'm sure you'd prefer Palztonk, right?"

John had had this talk with over a hundred demons in the past. If it were poker, he always had the nut. Not this time. The horrible uncertainty of playing from a weaker position eased caution into his reply. "So you're an old hand at this?"

"No." Her cheeks flushed. His eyes widened at the new experience moments before he slapped her face. He crossed her eyes and focused before smacking her face again.

Planning to pull a vial of holy water, John eased the emblem toward his satchel.

"Ot!"

The demonic syllable had multiple meanings, but from inflection and Mitzolkzka's fixed stare, John froze.

"My good, Representative," He crossed her hands over her knee. "That's not where you pulled it from."

A sickening, sweet, sticky film began to form on John's tongue. He drew a steadying breath to even his tone and bluffed. "I normally keep it there." John moved to put it back in his inner pocket. "No need to flex. We're still talking here."

Her cheeks and brow rose. The smile overtaking Beverly's face stretched beyond human expression. Her skin began to emit light like daytime-running headlights.

John kept his eyes from going to the door. It remained seven steps away–one step less than Mitzolkzka would have to take, yet four steps beyond what he could cover before the demon would be on him. Feeling the situation going to pot, John threw caution the wind and went all-in. "You know what happens to those who are forced out, right?"

"Something about being fed on by my fellow demons." Mitzolkzka stood. The shirt took on the demon's natural form, and a translucent body–the demon's true horned form–enveloped Beverly; within, her body hovered a foot from the ground.

"I hate when things get messy." John cursed inwardly and gripped the dagger. "Let's keep this clean, Mitzolkzka."

"Oh." Her smile twisted further. "Now you use my proper name?"

"Last chance." Adrenaline pumping, John curled and uncurled his toes inside his shoes to release some of his tension and to keep from bouncing in place. "Go now. Build up enough power to breech again, and come back through a proper venue."

"Tell me your true name, Representative. We both know it's not *Uncle John*." A prying glint sparked in her eyes. "I'd like to know who I'm dispatching to my always-ready-to-greet brethren."

John shook his head. "If you want me dead, you'll have to risk being booted by Bev for trying to kill a family member." He hoped the reminder would calm the situation.

Scattering the pillows, Mitzolkzka charged across the bed.

John swiped his thumb across his collar. He turned the knife to the ground and braced for the reverberating *bong* from the demon being repelled by powerful Palztonk wards.

The bong didn't happen.

Instead, an "eep" escaped John's mouth when Mitzolkzka grabbed him by the shoulder.

In what felt like one motion, the demon knocked the knife from his hand, ripped the satchel from his back, and hurled him further into the palatial room.

John tucked and rolled. Using the momentum, he rose to his feet and stumbled on a book bag.

Before he fell, Mitzolkzka gripped him by the throat. "You've served a demon, human."

John found himself hoisted from the ground.

"There's no Heaven for your kind."

Five

THE DEMON FORM WAS WARMER THAN THE HEATED rocks used at exclusive ritzy spas. The hotness of Mitzolkzka's breath was akin to a dry sauna. Brimstone worked John's nose while cotton candy continued to form on his tongue. Where others would be freaking out, John hoped for a shake.

"There's nothing for you do to, *Uncle John*." Mitzolkzka pointed to the stripped-away satchel. "Only your true name could possibly save you now."

"No."

The demon shook him.

A series of cracks and pops ran through his spine. John sighed.

Mitzolkzka growled.

Relief clung to his exhale. John traveled far and wide. No matter where he went, there wasn't a masseuse or chiropractor on the planet who could give a spinal adjustment half as well as a demon.

"Talk!"

John sighed, "Sorry."

Another shake elicited a few more cracks. John hooked his wrists over each other on the demon's forearm and lifted so he could talk. "That's good. Thanks."

Anger turned both Mitzolkzka's and Beverly's face. Both mouths bared sharp teeth at him.

John twisted his other wrist to let it slip past the lower one. The paper with Beverly's name on it was in his hand, which allowed it to pass through the demon form. With a deft turn of his wrist, John slid the paper across Beverly's arm.

It took half a second, but the demon's form burst like a bubble. Beverly's face contorted with Mitzolkzka's confusion. They dropped him, reeled away, and checked her forearm to inspect the damage.

"I know," John rubbed his neck and smiled. "Nearly negligible at first. Then comes the sting."

Unable to comprehend what just happened, Mitzolkzka became transfixed by John's hands, blinking Beverly's wide brown eyes in stunned disbelief.

"Your kind is so used to extremes. It makes you think that the slightest of cuts is a trick. Right now, you're convinced something worse is coming."

Mitzolkzka examined the cut expectantly.

"Well, you're wrong. Though they suck, they're not deadly." John presented the square. "It's what we call a paper cut."

Her arms lifted in excitement. "The Paper-Man!"

John took a tentative step back.

He'd never seen a demon convey such unbridled joy. The way their presence morphed human faces allowed for truly wicked expressions. That same elasticity applied to joyful expressions, but something about the raised cheeks revealing inhumanly long, well-fitted, sharp teeth edged on madness.

Thrilled, he imagined ice cream truck vendors felt this euphoric elation upon seeing thrilled children with fistfuls of cash and tiny, baby-toothed grins.

"I've heard about you, John Black." Mitzolkzka stood. "About you *and* your lovely paper."

"Really?" Prepared for a trick, John bent his knees so he could spring away if need be. "What have you heard?"

Mitzolkzka poked Beverly's cut and winced. "As weird as this may sound coming from one such as myself… nothing but good things."

John stayed ready. "Like what?"

"Like your willingness not to screw us over in spite of what we are to your kind." He extended Beverly's hand.

This was not the first time he had been recognized as *The Paper-Man*. Easing his stance, John took a cautionary step forward and handed over the small Post-It.

Mitzolkzka snatched the paper and regarded it with nothing short of reverence.

"It's almost like communion to you guys." John envisioned walking through a crowd of parting demons, piously distributing paper.

"Never done *communion*, but this is probably the closest." He toyed with the stickiness on the back. "Do you guarantee House Palztonk will let me broker passage through their safe zone if I return to Hell?"

John opened his mouth and paused.

A demon was asking for his word.

"As a representative of House Palztonk, appointed by Lou of said House, I extend the full courtesy of the house to aid you in the your next attempt to breech."

Mitzolkzka gave a momentary dubious look. "Good enough. Once I'm done with this, I'll head on back."

"Hold on." John grabbed her arm. The power crawling under her skin made the forearm feel like a jackhammer handle. "I'm here doing a job."

The demon switched the paper to the hand furthest away. "Yeah?"

"Don't just go." John stepped back. "I have to make it look like I did it."

Mitzolkzka gave a depraved grin.

John wasn't sure if the demon knew where this was heading, but his expression showed an interest if it were mutually beneficial.

He raised her eyebrows. "Yeah?"

"Look." Though no electronic devices worked around demons, John lowered his voice. "I'll give you another sheet if you follow my directions before leaving."

Mitzolkzka nodded her head and extended her hand. "You're okay in my book, Black."

Mike and Laura helped John as the three of them struggled to keep their possessed daughter in the steaming bathwater turned pink from hundreds of small cuts on her body.

Kicked away, John returned with force and drove Beverly's head underwater. "Be gone!"

Mitzolkzka's demon form expanded and cracked the tub before spiriting away in sizzling wisps of flame.

The cuts on Beverly's body started to heal, the tub repaired itself, and the gashes made on the three of them during the faux exorcism vanished.

John pulled Beverly to a sit. "It's…" He plopped back and leaned against the rapidly cooling bathroom tile. "It's done."

With a twinge of guilt, he watched the sobbing family cling to one another. Because of his showmanship, they would be closer now than ever before.

The nauseating feeling of a lie well told washed through him. He got to his feet.

Laura grabbed his wrist and pulled him into the family hug.

"Anything," Mike blathered. "Anything you need. Come to me, and it's yours."

John wanted to slide out of his skin.

"I mean that." Mike shook him. "Anything."

Nodding, John extricated himself. Leaving them to their moment. He gathered his things. Though he walked on two feet, the turning his gut made him want to crawl.

John made it to his car.

"Father!" Laura called as he was about to pull away. She jogged to the car and gave him a small business card. Then she dropped a small bag in his hand. "Thank you, Father. Thank you." She jogged back to the house where

Mike held Beverly wrapped in a blanket. The three went back to their family hug.

Scrawled across the back of the Schmidt Jewelers business card were the words *Anything you want, you get at cost.*

Dozens of small, glass-like sounds came from the pouch. Guilt tightened his muscles. Head lowered, John tossed the bag into the glove box and tried to disappear into his seat as he slunk away.

FROM ASHES

Las Vegas. Home to more lost souls per capita than any other city -- making it the brightest beacon on the material plane to Outsiders. Outsiders who want to come in…

John Black earns his living by pretending to be a priest so he gets the call to boot these uninvited guests.

No demon possession is standard, but something about this one prompts John into lowering his guard. Will he survive?

ONE

Knives in place, I laced my boots tight over my jeans. I stood, closed my eyes, and took in a last few deep breaths of the peach-scented oxygen. Though faint and false, it's the best perk of the Svalbard shelter and a wonderful reminder of how things used to be.

Picking up my mask, I placed the cool, hard plastic over my mouth and slid the elastic over my head. Pressing it against my face, I took three sharp breaths. The seal took. Now the air smelled and tasted like Tupperware that may have once stored fruit cocktail. The slit in the thick translucent latex separating the small *dress* dome from *vacuum-1* resisted as I pressed through.

Pham stopped her pacing and pivoted the other side of the clear membrane to face me. The hood on her cotton long-sleeve coat swung like a small cape. Head shaved bald, she wiped her head down at the end of the day instead of having anything that could impede her peripheral vision. She slid her AK47 behind her and fanned her arms in quick, small circles to hurry me out.

Scooping my goggles, I pushed through the other side of *vacuum-1*. "What?"

She grabbed and twisted my collar to pull me down to her five-foot eye level. Her mask pressed against my neck and, angry, her Thai accent nipped at her words. "You have to tell them, Don."

"I did." She released me, but I stayed close. Partly to keep our voices low, but mostly because this is the closest we have been in weeks. I dared to edge closer. "They flat out refuse not to wear them."

Her eyes shifted over my shoulder. "They're going to get us killed." She pushed me away. A practiced shrug rolled her gun forward as she stalked from the shelter.

"Donald, is there–" I turned. Colette was directly behind me in her grey Svalbard Seed Vault jumpsuit with the high-end SSV respirator helmet in place. She pointed to Pham's shadow beyond the white exterior and switched to French. "–a problem with our guard leader?"

"No." Her hazel eyes were hidden beyond the orange visor. The HUD within probably already alerting her of the rise in my body temperature from my flushed skin, and that I had lied. My tongue slid across the tasteless hard plastic when I wetted my lips. I took a small step away from her.

Colette grabbed my hand, closing more distance than I had placed between us. "What is wrong?"

Beyond her, Archibald moved in the dress dome. Though I understood her, I kept to English. "It's your guys' gear." I twisted my hand, but she held on. "That might be standard wear around The Vault, but out here, it paints us as targets."

"Want me to take it off–" Her head tilted, and I imagined her eyes half-closed beyond the visor. "–again?"

Archibald stood.

I twisted and pulled my hand free. She might have already cost me my marriage, but I wasn't going to let her possibly spoil this, too. To her, it's a game, but if we couldn't get the Svalbard seeds to germinate here, the world was worse than anyone knew.

Having slid the goggles over my head, I let them slap over my sockets. "Listen, while I can't keep you two from wearing SSV gear, this will be the last time we erect the pavilion."

Her shoulders and hips shifted slightly as she stepped in, making me aware of my poor choice of words. Colette pressed her body against me. She was soft and ample where my Pham was taut and lean. "Should we just *erect* a single tent instead?"

I batted her hands away from my jeans and motioned my head toward Archibald. "Have you told him?"

She turned to see his hand coming through and, before his helmeted head pressed through, Colette had moved back to the other side of the *gear* dome to greet him.

"Tell him." I turned so he would not see where my body was hottest. Pushing through the final slit, I lifted the flap and moved out onto the ashen earth to find my wife in the miasma.

In the past, from here, I could see the lush Albay Gulf and the deep blue oceans beyond, but we hadn't had a clear day since the deadline had past.

Man's Folly, a new terrorist group, started making demands through the net. Worldwide nuclear disarmament topped their list. They did not threaten or say why. They simply gave a completion date. When the day came, the Internet was alive with chatter and speculation, but the day ended without event.

Memes of national capital buildings started floating around social media. Above the buildings, in bold *Man's Folly*. Below, emboldened, italicized, and in quotes *Or what?* As though in reply, they pirated local affiliate feeds to show their members simultaneously dropping two dozen bombs into an equal number of volcanoes around the world.

Walking around the Svalbard pavilion, I found Pham standing near the edge of vision–a little over hundred feet–among the rest of our diminished guard. The four men, slightly taller than she, looked down at the ground as she drew with a stick. The edges of my goggles had collected a thin line of the fine soot before I made it to them. My exposed skin, forehead, and cheeks started to feel a bit heavy. Having been licked by the summer humidity of the Philippines, I was gathering ash.

Pham's now grey bald head indicated how my face may have looked. She was speaking to them in Mandarin, a language they all had in common, as she moved the stick north on the impromptu landscape before dragging the tip east. Though I missed the setup and did not understand an inch of Chinese, I could tell they were planning our trek.

The newest guy, a local we had contact with before Man's Folly existed, modified her line, cutting the northward movement in half. He said something that had all of them nodding in agreement.

She looked at me. Her deep brown eyes guarded her emotions, but the small knot between her eyebrows signaled she did not want me in her sight. "Jon says the area has broken down into little fiefdoms with different warlords proclaiming themselves King, President, or something similar." Sparing me, she returned her gaze to the ground. "Like in times of old, everyone has become fiercely territorial and distrustful of others."

Though only imaginary, I think I can feel the ash draw into my lungs with each burnt inhale as I speak. "It's survival. It does that."

Pham's eyes returned to me and, for a moment, I registered accusation and pain. "It is truly sad when food is more plentiful than trust."

Tuk, Pham's brother, translated, and they nodded. He met my eye, but before I could wonder if she had told him, his face adjusted. His cheeks rose, smiling behind the mask. His gaze went past me. Tuk's smile dropped a moment before he raised his gun and Colette's scream sliced through the air.

Two

Pham pivoted, kicking up ash as she went from crouching to sprinting before I could pull my pistol.

The Svalbard pavilion, a single large dome from outside, was covered in overnight ash, its outline barely distinguishable through the haze at this distance. Larger pieces of debris kicked up by John and the other guards as they passed me peppered my shins.

A low growl rolled from ahead. Colette's small, helmeted form stood behind Archibald, who held a stick between them and a snarling dog. Half extended, he jabbed to keep the canine at bay instead of taking it down.

Pham hooted when it shifted weight to its hind legs. We added hoots to hers. Instead of springing on Archibald, the dog assessed us, rushing for a moment before bolting away.

Tuk and the guards who had come on land with us turned to chase after the dog. Jon stopped to take in the shelter and stare at the two in SSV gear.

Pham barked Chinese at Jon while pointing to the ground. Jon went in a line away from camp, following tracks. The ash pronounced the tracks. Even with my limited skill, I could see where it came from and which direction it ran. If the dog rested for a moment, we would have a feast tonight.

The warm air inside my mask was thick from exertion and, as the collected moisture ran down my cheeks, a bitter smell came through. I looked to where the dog had been and then to Archibald. The front and inside of his grey jumpsuit, from the crotch down, had darkened.

Pulling a *my hero*, Colette tried to nestle into him when he turned, but he shrugged her off and slid back into the pavilion.

Capitalizing on the moment, I pushed into the gear dome and pulled my mask away to wipe the collected moisture away. "We have to break this down, Doctor." Just seeing the dog made my stomach rumble. I pulled my tin of shredded jerky and tamped it. "The sooner, the better." Careful not to spill a flake from the eighty-dollar can, I cracked the top and slid a pinch between my cheek and gum – the smoked chipotle mercifully masked the natural flavor of whatever kind of meat was unable to escape the canner. "Dogs don't range far or last long anymore."

He did not respond.

"You hear me talking?"

"Uh, um, yes. Soon." Though Norse, his English was shamefully flawless – under normal circumstances. That was the second stammer I had heard from him since we met at The Vault. The first splutter came during dinner, when he was assigned as the SSV's spokesperson to the outside world. Charged with making pacts with those in command of hydroponics or land not poisoned by Man's Folly's second phase, to begin re-growth.

On the boat, Archibald used the projector from his helmet to aid his explanation of how they had turned ninety-five percent of the planet barren, but science was never my thing. If I would have stayed for the lecture, I would not have been alone.

I closed the tin and put it back inside my coat. "Try to make that *soon* sooner."

His zipper sounded. "Will do."

I nodded to his form beyond *vacuum-1*. Scraping the caked ash away from the border it had made around my mask, I heard harsh whispers outside.

Jesus, it was just Pham and Colette out there. Their forms, visible through the exterior wall, were close.

Mask back in place, I took three rapid breaths, and the seal took. I stepped out. Colette cradled herself against me. Her helmet thumped against my chest, keeping her long blonde hair inside from trailing down my arms.

Though not part of the original escort deal, the SSV consortium paid handsomely for us to take Colette on Archibald's mission. They told me her helpless demeanor had won her access to the secluded sanctuary, but her *ways* brought trouble and disharmony. They did not elaborate, but the dried fruit packs and money were too good to turn down.

The first night on the boat, I experienced the kind of trouble she must have caused every married man in The Vault. Her habits and sexual appetite got us booted from Taal before we had a chance to meet their grand poobah.

Behind her, my wife made a hard pushing motion - directing me to shove Colette away. From the angle, she strongly preferred that I send the temptress to the ground.

Her perfume, a bouquet of soft flowers, slipped through my mask, and my head swam. I couldn't shove her, but I tried to untangle her arms. She bested me at each twist and turn. "Off."

Pham swiped her thumb under her chin and left the direction Jon had gone. That usually meant someone was off the crew. Since Colette was part of the mission, a shudder rippled through my body as what she probably meant.

Seeing my angry wife disappear into the haze, I jammed a hand between our bodies, pushing Colette's helmet and threatening to drive it from her head. My words came through clenched teeth. "Get off."

"Donald, I can see your heat." She pressed her pelvis up into me. "You wouldn't."

"I would." I brought my other hand between our bodies, snaking it between her cleavage.

She loosened at the prospect.

"And I am." A quick turn of both wrists and both my hands were on her shoulders. I hooked her ankle with my heel and did what I should have done that first night.

She uttered a surprised yelp before she thumped on the earth, sending a cloud of ash from the ground. Before she could collect herself, I took off after my wife.

The two sets of human tracks were easier to follow than the dogs.

I didn't have to go far before I found them. Her bald head denoted her body, and she was disturbingly close to his hooded form; both leaned toward the other.

Darkness started to swell in my chest, and my hand inched toward my desert eagle as I got a taste of what my Pham must have been feeling.

She slid him a pouch. He nodded. They shook hands and turned to come back to camp. Upon being seen, instead of being her ever-ready self, Pham froze. I had finally managed to sneak up on her.

Jon, on the other hand, leveled his submachine gun at me.

THREE

MY BLADDER QUIVERED, MY COLON RUMBLED, and my sphincter tightened hard enough to break a pencil.

Pham dropped to a knee and raised her gun.

My breath left my chest, filling my mask with a warm, smoky scent.

She yelled, "Papa. Hotel."

Fear locked my joints and clouded my mind. I was at a loss. Then I drew half a breath as the friend or foe verification process registered. "Alpha Mike."

She lowered her weapon and tapped Jon's leg while standing. "What are you doing, Don?"

My breathing returned to normal and I swallowed the chipotle-flavored saliva which had pooled in my mouth. "I could ask the same thing, Love."

"*Love?*" Her voice rose, making the word two fuming syllables as she started marching toward me. "*Love?*" she called again as she closed on me and pushed me back with her force and momentum.

I fell, and ash rose as she kicked at me.

"You don't get to use that word no more." Her accent flared, signaling her hurt since I could not see her face clearly through the disturbed ground. "Not toward me."

I spun as she circled to kick my torso and managed to keep the assault concentrated on my legs. "I'm sorry!"

"Sorry?" She'd yelled before, but the question came out in a rare scream.

For a moment, I was glad she stopped kicking. Then my guts tightened when I realized she had taken a step back and I could only see below her knees. Her feet were slightly apart, the right foot in front of her left, supporting most of her weight. She's stood that way on the edges of boats, walls, and cliffs. It was the stance she took before firing down. Then I remembered her swinging her thumb under the throat.

I lowered my head and extended my hands palm up as I had when I knelt to propose to her in Sri Lanka.

Instead of being riddled with bullets, I was speckled with dirt before she stalked away.

Not sure if she had gone with the better choice, I laid flat on my back and waited for the ash to settle.

When I got back to camp, the Svalbard pavilion had been automated and had just finished breaking itself down. It now appeared to be a very cumbersome backpack instead of a high-tech dormitory.

"Jon says the highway is full of traps." As though nothing had happened, Pham walked close, her voice calm and her accent nearly unnoticeable. "He says

Bonga is the friendliest route. We'll have to beg a bit and give three tributes, but we'll be able to pass through."

Scanning the area, Jon was with the other guards. "I don't know. Did you see the way he stopped and stared at the SSV gear?" In case he had audio enhancers, I turned my back toward him, lowered my voice, and spoke Thai. "He's new. Do you think we can trust him?"

She cut her eyes when I said *trust* and walked away.

I sucked at the jerky, drawing on the smoky flavor as I considered our options. If the roads were trapped, whoever set them probably had a radar relay to detect when someone tried to navigate the stretch of road. Worst-case scenario, the radar would guide weapons, and we would be shelled or blasted before we knew it.

Colette's flowery scent carried on the slight breeze as she and Archibald approached. She clung to his arm, his elbow held tight against her side.

He asked, "And so?"

"Well." I pointed the direction the Captain had given us when he set us on land. "There's certain death." I turned and motioned vaguely toward where Bonga might be. "And there's possible death." My shoulders rose and dropped. Deep down, it registered: I didn't care to live anymore. Against everything I would normally do, I gave him the choice. "Decision is yours to make."

The worst part about their helmets was not being able to see their expressions. "If it is all the same, I would like to go with *possible death*, please."

"Possible death it is." I motioned to Pham, relaying our direction to her.

She clapped, handed Tuk a bag, and started following Jon, taking point with him as we started toward Bonga. Tuk and the other two came back to join me in escorting Archibald and Colette – in case we were overtaken from behind or if a pack of scavengers come across us.

One of his arms was occupied, so I handed Tuk my small pack and hefted the compacted pavilion onto my back. It was surprisingly light, but awkward.

+

Pham stood with Jon on a platform as he yelled Tagalong into the haze. High above the ground in the miasma, a light bell rang. They adjusted, looking from where they had been yelling their answers to where the new questions came from.

Ricky was translating for us. Whoever guarded Bonga had concern because Jon was from Bacacay. For his part, Jon was swearing on his ancestors' souls that the recent happenings of his home city had nothing to do with him, as he had been away on an escort mission.

Tuk tapped my arm and gave me a small pouch – about the same size as the one Pham had given him. I searched his face for clues, but, like mine, his mouth was hidden by the mask. His eyes were passive, almost indifferent.

Did he know what was inside, or was he running another errand for his sister without asking?

Either way, I took the bag.

Ricky said, "Jon's waving us on."

The bell rang again and everyone started to move forward as I opened the pouch.

I tried to take a step, but, upon seeing the contents, I fell to my knees.

Four

ALL OF THE GOOD FLAVOR FROM MY PINCH OF JERKY was gone and the remaining meat started to fill my mouth with a sour tang that was either rat, human, or something else equally toxic. I looked forward to getting inside so I could spit it out. Bonga was once a very colorful city, but had taken on the same muted tones as the rest of the world. Playing some form of tag, kids ran and screamed after each other with less than adequate masks for the amount of ash in the air.

The Cardinal, as the ruler of Bonga wanted to be called, made the elementary school his castle. The bell rang six times as we brought up the rear and entered. Censers burned sandalwood incense, and crosses were affixed along the wall a foot apart. Ricky explained both were to bar evil spirits. Beneath them, the wall was canvassed with old school projects, most covered with too much soot to make out.

His throne, a leather high-backed chair–probably from the principal's office–was at the far end of the gymnasium with twenty men armed with machine guns between us. "Why, on God's gray earth, should I let you pass through my city?"

The chairs presented were made to seat Asian children. Since his court customs barred standing while speaking to him, I took a knee. "My good and just Cardinal, when we told our Captain of our destination, he assured me of your generous nature."

He sat straighter in his chair and nodded. "I am known for my generosity."

"As much as you give…" I extend my hands and showed they were empty. Keeping my moves slow, I reached into Tuk's backpack. Several of the guns pointed at us were racked to remind me of their presence. "It could only behoove your people if you have more to give." Gripping two sleeves of N95 filter masks, I pulled them out and presented them. "For your people."

He motioned a lazy hand. One of the nearest gunmen moved forward, took them, and retreated. "What else?"

"For your table…" I lifted a large bag of beans and freeze-dried vegetables.

These barely earned a finger raise. The same gunman retrieved these items and set them next to the masks. He smiled from his throne and pointed. "For my third gift, I choose that small pouch dangling from your belt loops."

"Cardinal, I can guarantee you what I have planned for my third tribute is better than the pouch."

The gift retriever had set his gun down and brandished a knife on his way over. The Cardinal shifted in his chair and rolled his hands in anticipation. "The pouch will suffice." Once the strings were cut, he called, "Bring it to me."

Archibald whispered, "What is in there?"

I shook my head and watched the shine leave the Cardinal's eyes as he dipped a finger into the pouch to make sure he wasn't missing anything.

"What was your third gift going to be?"

I opened my zip-up and pointed to my desert eagle. "No finer way to a put hole in someone."

"I'll take that instead."

He handed the pouch back to the carrier, who walked it over and placed it in my hand. I looked at Pham as he unsnapped the gun and pulled it from the holster.

She took a breath and averted her eyes.

The Cardinal stood when the runner delivered the gun to him.

I asked, "Do we have your permission to move through?"

"What's in the tin next to your holster?"

I opened my hoodie again as the carrier started back over. "An extra gift, my Liege, dried and smoked meat." Tonguing the foul pinch forward, I showed it. The smell rolled to my nose, and I quickly pushed it back before the runner got too close. Once he was on his way back, I added, "I would hate to part with it, but if you want it-"

"I do."

"Then it is yours."

He sat and set the gun on his lap to accept the tin. "For this, I will tell you, if you are heading to Mayon

Planetarium, they never give anything to foreigners."
The Cardinal moved his hand in an arc toward Jon.
"Have him speak for you."

I bowed. "Thank you for the advice."

He gave a courtly nod. "You have my leave."

+

I waited until we were out of eyesight from Bonga before
I raised my mask and spat the rancid meat out. The mild
exposure would not do as much damage as swallowing.
It was easy to put the mask just inside the caked lines on
my cheeks to get it to seal again.

Having her helmet back on, Colette finally stopped
whining about us putting ash in her hair.

"It's about a day and half hike." Jon took to walking,
and we all started moving.

This time, Pham hung back and Tuk walked point
with him.

+

We moved and set camp in silence. The rest of the
group took cues from Pham and I. The Svalbard
pavilion kept the shape of a backpack as we unrolled
our sleeping bags.

Archibald and Colette looked ridiculous sleeping
with their heads outside of their bags. It was warm
enough that they really didn't need the bags since,

with their helmets on, they had nothing to fear from the environment.

Pham and I were on first watch, but we kept an eye on the darkness without saying a word.

Before going to bed, I extended my hand to her.

She did not take it. I like to think she didn't see it.

I roused to a single loud thunk. It was almost like a shovel's first bite into earth. I peeked out of my bag. Ricky sat near the edge of my vision. Jon, the second sentry, was nowhere to be found. My hand instinctively went to where my desert eagle used to rest and closed on air. I whispered. "Pham? Tuk?"

Tuk replied, "What was that noise?"

"Don't know." I unzipped further. "Ricky, what was that?" He didn't move. Voice at near normal volume, I repeated, "Ricky."

Tuk slid from his bag and crept toward Ricky. I rolled out of mine but stayed on my hands and knees to survey the sleepers. There were four bodies in bags, but only Archibald's helmeted head was in place.

My head shook. Colette was shameless. To slip out of bed to seduce the sentry was the height was selfishness and put everyone at risk. The only question on my mind was did she do Ricky first, or was he waiting his turn.

I paused. There was a bag with a body where Colette had gone to sleep. Near where the head was supposed to be was a dark blotch on the ground.

"Everybody up!" Tuk yelled, "Ricky's dead!"

Not close enough to verify, Pham called from a ways behind me, "So is Colette!"

FIVE

Tuk poked Pham, and she jabbed her finger back at him. The two Thais were purposefully speaking Chinese to keep me out of the loop. Chang, our remaining guard, tried to be the calm voice between the siblings.

My mouth still had the taste of the shredded jerky, but the scent that came to my nose was Colette's flowery bouquet with its dizzying effect. She pressed her chest against my back. "What are they arguing about?"

Pham and Tuk fell silent.

I rolled away from her and looked to where she had come from. She was the helmeted one where Archibald had gone to sleep. Which meant–

My throat tightened at the fear of what I was going to find. I scrambled to where Colette had laid down for the night and unzipped the bag. There, from the neck down, was Archibald. Our main chance at righting the world again lay dead. A long, reinforced and sharpened sheet of metal was discarded near our site.

Tuk poked Pham again and spoke Chinese. I recognized Jon's name. He repeated the same sentence and she barked back, motioning to Colette.

"Guys!" I started to roll up my bag. "We need to get out of here. When whoever killed Archibald for his helmet gets to where he is going, they are going to come back for more valuables."

Zippers rasped, cloth flapped, and elastic snapped.

Not used to breaking camp, Colette was the slowest. She stepped back when Tuk and Chang jumped in to do it for her.

Pham crossed her arms and shook her head at the spectacle.

I stood. "Colette, we're going to need that helmet."

"What?" Colette inched away. "No. It's mine. The Vault gave it to me."

"It's a matter of survival." I moved closer. "That helmet probably has logistic features that'll help us get to the planetarium before the killers come back."

"It wouldn't fit you." She continued moving back. "Your head is too big."

Behind me, Pham belted, "Move, Don!" I did and turned to see her pointing the AK47 at Colette. She was in her killing stance. "Do you think I will hesitate if I have to kill you for that?"

Colette stopped moving. "His head's too big."

"Mine isn't." Pham moved in. "Give it to me."

I threw the Svalbard shelter on my back, shrugged on Archibald's pack.

Pham stopped ten feet from Colette. "Take it off, set it down, and back away."

"Then I won't have a mask." Colette protested.

"You can wear mine." Pham said as she aimed the gun at Colette's gut. "You've already tried everything else that's mine."

She took off the helmet and set it on the ground. The perfume filled the area.

Pham removed her mask and tossed it to Colette. "Move."

Weak-kneed and wobbly, Tuk got to his feet. "Why don't you leave her alone?"

"Yeah." Chang agreed but failed to get to his feet.

Colette smiled as she clasped her wrists and Pham fell over sideways. She held Pham's mask to her face as she sashayed toward my incapacitated wife, the strap holding the discarded AK47 at her side. "He was mine long before he was yours."

My stomach lurched and I nearly blacked out. On my knees, I dug in the pouch and pulled out the earbud and jammed the Man's Folly transmitter in. The wooziness induced by her subsonic bracelets subsided. My hand gripped a boot knife, but before I could do what I wanted, I froze. Familiar voices called out.

"Donnie, is that you?"

"Are you back in the link?"

"The hive has missed you."

Colette nodded, dropping the mask and opening her arms for an embrace. "Your Queen has missed you."

My memories began to fuzz around the edges. What I could not recall prior to meeting Pham started to come into focus as life with my wife began to fade.

The closer Colette came, the stronger her pheromones. Life with Pham was hard. Memories of how easy life was under Colette's guidance painted the difference.

"Yes." I replied to the voices. "I'm back." They cheered when I looked at Colette. "I've missed you, too."

She stood over me. Her hazel eyes drank me in anew as she let her hair down. "Come home, honey."

I looked to Pham. Ash from the ground highlighted the trail of her tears like the Mahaweli River we cruised during our honeymoon.

Popping the earbud from my ear, I spun as I rose to my feet. Blade drawn, I swung it under Colette's chin. Blonde hair fell in the ash as I came back to the ground from the effort.

She grabbed at the deep, bloody gash, trying to stem the flow, but it was a lost cause. Colette dropped to her knees, gripping her throat as we locked eyes. A deadly, unspoken command sparked from her eyes and a part of me that I had forgotten–a part of me that she controlled completely–obeyed.

We both flopped on the barren ash-clad earth we made.

+

I came to on a pillowtop bed. The walls and ceiling of the room were painted a deep blue. Glow-in-the-dark stars, ranging from an eighth of an inch to two inches wide, displayed how the night sky looked before I joined Man's Folly and helped ruin the Earth. I tried to call out, but my mouth was dry. My throat constricted, and a hiss of air escaped.

Pham was holding my hand and she gripped it tight; her beautiful black hair had grown out. "Shhh. It's okay."

Remembering Archibald being decapitated, my eyes started to water and I shook my head.

"Yes, it is." She rubbed an ice chip between my lips and, like she had applied oil, I was able to open. "The scientists here were able to figure out the pavilion and found the seeds sewn into the Svalbard Seed Vault suits."

The ice chip started to melt on my tongue, but it was not turning into water faster than the weight of sleep.

"With their volcanic soil and the seeds from The Vault, they can grow plants." She stroked my forehead.

A trickle dripped down my esophagus and when I cleared my throat, it was like I had swallowed sandpaper.

"Relax, baby." She kissed my forehead.

As much as I wanted to do what she said, I cleared my throat again on the next trickle. I was tired and going to fade. Before I did, I managed a faint, "I love you."

TIME LOOP

Looking back on the past rarely compares to one's memories. Having been a punk, Terrance Lee failed to realize he let the bastards grind him.

Howard found him at work. Under Howard's wild-eyed gaze, the tie around Terrance's neck feels like a choker collar and the employee-of-the-year watch on his wrist burns.

When Howard offers a chance to return to their glory days, how could Terrance say no?

TIME LOOP

HAVING STOOD ON THIS SPOT MANY TIMES IN HIS youth, Terrance Lee inhaled deeply to take in the crisp chill of a Vegas winter night and the view of a 1993 Las Vegas Strip. Besides not being able to have this vantage point from atop the Dunes hotel, the entire city felt like an undercooked-cake-batter version of the Vegas he lived in.

All the basic ingredients were there and it had been cooking for a while, but things had yet to rise.

The time jump left his nose clear, but a thick, piney residue formed on his tongue. Drawing it into a glob, he walked to the edge. Terrance leaned over, opened his mouth, and let it fall.

He lost it in the dark but found the people traffic amazing. Tourists walked the strip–in massive herds–across Flamingo. Man, he forgot how long tourists would continue to walk against the light.

Horns honked.

Birds were flipped.

A taxi driver revved his engine.

Two belligerent drunks blocked the right lane, making traffic go around them.

"That's right," Terrance cheered the cab, which barely swerved wide enough to avoid them.

The city hadn't had enough of tourist fatalities yet. It would, but the sky-bridges were still a few years away.

Twenty-four stories used to be the tallest on the strip. In his native future-time, this wasn't even a quarter of the height of the Stratosphere.

"Oh man!" For some reason, seeing the Maxim made him remember Vegas World. The first casino to boast one hundred times odds, Terrance turned to where the Stratosphere Tower would rise into the sky to find Stupak's folly. Treasure Island stood in the way. He exhaled his disappointment at not seeing Vegas World. "Oh, man."

He turned one-eighty to face the Tropicana.

The distant desert looked kind of naked without the New York New York, the green glow of the MGM on the clouds, and the light from the Luxor penetrating the sky.

Pine-slime started to form on the back of his tongue.

Terrance faced west. The sprawl came nowhere near the Red Rocks. If he remembered right, Spanish Trails would still be the furthest community out that way. Pressed against the laughable outer limits of Durango Drive.

He couldn't count the streets to be precise, but the dark of the desert meeting city streetlights indicated his memory was close to the mark.

Howard-of-the-far-future had really sent him back.

The thin layer on his tongue started to give off a smell that crawled into his nose through his nasal cavity.

His sinuses started to slowly close.

"What the hell, man?" Terrance became stuffy. He complained to the black device tight around his wrist, made to look like and old-fashioned Swatch watch. "You know pine kicks off my allergies."

Howard-of-the-far-future's hologram did not appear.

Terrance shook his wrist and tapped the device. "Howie?"

Three toots of air horns honed his attention into a fine focus. Three beams of lights bopping along the golf course signaled he, Howie, and Fred were celebrating successfully sneaking onto the property.

Two security carts sped from the building toward the light and sound.

They tossed their flashlights back over the fence, dropped their air horns, and hid out in a sand trap.

Terrance scanned the south golf course.

Members of the Sixth Street Gang were out there somewhere.

Howard-of-the-far-future only wanted him to deliver a message and the Swatch-device to Howie-of-the-past. Saving Fred's life would happen on a subsequent trip.

However, if he did everything right, he could do that and also keep Fred Castle from dying on this jump.

+

Terrance spat the pine-slime more often, but his nose closed just the same. He massaged his sinuses as he crept into the old gift shop where he had discovered Mentos as a preteen. A hundred feet away sat his second-favorite arcade for hustling tourist kids out of their quarters.

Howard said the best place to chat him up would be in the north tower.

However, this would be where he hid to score the first hit of the night and fastest double-elimination in their history of paintballing. Even with Howard using his almost-cheating Rapide.

The device on his wrist did more than time travel. It also improved his vision in the dark, but it paled in comparison to the night goggles Howard made for them back in the day.

The memory gave him pause. Why was the night-sight so shitty?

He smacked his forehead and gritted his teeth at the sound.

As teens, they wore the goggles. This device lay on his wrist and still affected his vision. A smile spread his lips as he recalled Howie's exasperated replies when he asked for more in the past. "Hold on," Howie would say. "I'll have it go pick up your comics, too."

Terrance pressed his lips together and worked them side to side.

He and Howie had gone separate ways after Fred's funeral. Perhaps the memory of how Howie used to be–how they used to all be–made him agree to go back in time.

The nicknames.

The games.

The songs.

It was a glorious time and worth something.

Though the liquidation took care of the slot machines and table games in the Dunes, as it did then, he marveled again at the amount of furnishings and cabinetry still intact. Though Wynn had bigger plans for the property, he could have converted it into Vegas's first indoor paintball field.

A person, a shadow barely discernable against the deeper darkness behind it, crept into the gift shop. The silhouette of a ponytail dangled between his arm and torso as he got into position.

Terrance rubbed his receding hairline. Man, he missed that long hair.

He kept his voice low. "Hey. Terry."

"What?" Terry turned, gun pointed. "Who's there?"

"First, listen. Okay?"

"Fuck you, bum."

Terry's body pivoted from behind the counter and ran into the darkness.

Listening to the footsteps fade toward the Arcade, Terrance stared at the spot where he had been in his youth.

He recalled being a bit of a jerk, but apparently his sister nailed it–he was a complete asshole.

Terrance spat the pine-slime and exhaled his relief.

In his memory, he didn't talk to anyone and still had the fastest double-elimination.

This slice of time was no longer his past.

His fists pumped the air.

Howard insisted Terrance listened to him drone on about his Prevailing Quantum-Relativity of a Singular Timeline theory. As it turned out, the genius MIT super-graduate had been wrong. Terrance figured changing the past would be like *Sliding Doors*–not *Back to the Future*– and he was right.

Feeling unburdened, he began to imagine what kind of killing he could make with Magic the Gather-ing cards, VeriSign stock, and decades of fairly accurate sport champion game picks. Things he planned to tell his younger self when they were the same person.

Confident, he stood. Then leaned against the glass case where he first discovered Jolt Cola.

On top of his congestion, a migraine stabbed from both temples.

His equilibrium fled.

The room rocked one direction, making him shift his feet to stay upright, and then slammed the opposite way.

A third shot of pain lit smack-dab at the center of his forehead.

It came from outside his skull.

Everything went dark.

+

Of the three pains, the banging forehead remained.

He put his hand to his forehead.

Pulse!

He pulled it away and set his mind against doing so again.

His equilibrium returned; he tried to sit up and found the left side of his face glued to the floor.

Terrance put his hands next to his face. One landed in something wet and sort of slick. The other pressed into something thick and extremely sticky; he lifted that hand.

While out, his throat had started to close. He drew air in from the tight stream.

To clear his throat, he forced air out.

He could breathe better, but a gummy-syrup covered the back of the hand next to his mouth.

"Eaah!" He pushed against the floor to free himself.

His cheek resisted.

Rolling his face with steady pressure freed him from the pool of hardened slime.

His tongue no longer registered the taste.

The fluid coming from his forehead followed an established path down along his left nostril. It held a slight stickiness when it dried between his fingers. The stuff coming from his tongue was thicker now. Resinous.

While unconscious, a layer had hardened, bonding the side of his tongue to his upper teeth.

"Fulk." He tried to cuss.

Without full use of his tongue, the profanity came out mushy and wrong. It reminded him of his grandmother, who managed to survive four strokes before the fifth one took her.

Not remembering how much of which fluid got on his hands, Terrance kept his fingers spread apart.

He wanted to try and pull his tongue free, but a possibility–his fingers getting stuck on his tongue–kept his hands from trying to fix his mouth.

His forehead lit with pain when he frowned at the idea, which made him furrow, which eased the ache. A vicious cycle of agony continued as he wanted to frown and the pain made him ease his expression. An uneasy balance between furrowed and not played on his forehead.

Sinuses were the least of his problems.

Howard did not tell him he would take on a death sentence when he chose to jump.

All of that bullshit about the MIT super-grad not interacting with himself was just a tangled web of lies to get him to believe Howard could not be in the candidate pool.

Terrance did his best not to frown, but did.

The balancing agony act started again.

Howard-of-the-far-future did not smell like pine, and he didn't have the same growing gunk problem that Terrance hand.

Time travel wasn't a death sentence.

The third angle, the sharpest of their best friend triangle, was trying to kill him.

The clap of compressed air lit in the distance.

Terrance struggled to his feet.

His equilibrium came and went as two sets of memories fought to occupy the same block of time in his past. One set, the one he wanted to believe, had him scoring a double-elimination on his friends.

The more agreeable recollection featured him running from a bum in the dark. In this one, he almost ran into Howie coming from Keno. As they battled it out in the wide corridor, Fred shot them both from cover in the arcade. Scoring the fastest doubled elimination.

Since his younger self was an asshole, and he the bum, Terrance knew the second had to be right.

Yet a part of him, perhaps an unknown deep-down desire for glory, struggled to hold onto the other set.

The timeline along his unrealistic remembrance had them hearing weird hoots and going to continue their matches in the north tower.

In reality, they went to the north tower to get away from a bum Terry had woken up in the gift shop.

Willing to cling mightily to the less likely of the two, Terrance realized Fred died in that one, too.

Useless, he relented to certainty and let the fabrication fade.

His forehead still pulsed from when he had tripped and knocked his head on the cooler door handle, but his equilibrium returned.

Head pounding, he beat feet to the north tower.

+

The bottom of his tongue started collecting the slime. He hoped his taste buds were done, but the rear right side of his tongue still offered a square centimeter of sensitivity. It served as a reminder of the constant pine-doom collecting, growing, in his mouth.

As long as he spat, he was good.

With half his throat lost for intake, Terrance became lightheaded as he took the stairs. He had come down with altitude sickness in Denver, and this felt just like that.

Why did they always play on the seventeenth floor?

The pulsing headache teamed up with the light-headedness at the tenth flight when he stopped to spit.

He rounded the fifteenth floor and worked at staying upright.

A flurry of shots echoed to him from further up the stairwell.

Constantly spitting left his throat dry.

He thought of the gloop as his mother had taught him to think of mucus when sick–better out than in.

Terrance rounded another flight of stairs and spat.

A flat shot, the kind that putters the paintball a few feet instead of a few hundred, echoed from the open stairwell one flight up.

Someone being out of CO_2 meant blitzing them.

Footfalls were rapidly approaching his end of the hallway.

One of the three hit the stairwell, which was against the rules. Someone cheated.

Taking the stairs four at a time, his younger self came down the flight.

He wanted to call himself on it, but more was at stake. Remembering he always like to round the landings wide, Terrance moved against the wall, hoping to be in the way.

"Shit." Terry had too much momentum to stop.

Terrance grabbed his arm and shouted his secret nickname. "Raphael!"

With a twist and a low spin, his younger self slipped out of the cheap Members Only jacket he bought at Savers just for paintballing. A quick stutter step and Terry slid through the door to the sixteenth floor.

Terrance had forgotten for a moment how athletic he was, and it cost him his last chance to corner himself.

"Fulk. Fulk. Fulk."

He tried to pull the coat from his hand, only to have it stick to the goop.

Giving in to the throbbing headache, Terrance sat on the stairs. Was he wrong? He stopped and checked his memory of the night for the bum.

Nope. The bum did not pop out at him again.

Howard had used him and tried to kill him. No way was he going to relay the message of future glory to Howie.

He would not stop to listen to himself, so he could not tell himself how to get rich and live well.

When he thought about the past again, he actually went looking for the bum, but could not find him.

Something Fred said sent him searching.

Terrance's eyes sprung wide open.

Thrilled, he tolerated the pain as used the coat on the handrail to hoist himself back into action.

Like his family did when he turned to selling drugs during his college years, Terrance wrote his younger self off and focused purely on the new goal.

Saving Fred.

+

Terrance leaned his back against the wall and peeked down the hallway. With what he remembered of Fred's play style, he also camped–which was why it would have been awesome to be the one with the double-elimination.

He spat a glob.

The square centimeter section of bare taste buds became little more than a pinpoint of pine.

The question would be, since Fred had already bagged a double-elim, would he be on the hunt to boost his kill count or had he posted up for another spectacular splatting?

No way to know, but one thing would remain constant: they all stepped on the center of the thresholds as, reinforced by doorjambs, the sweet spot kept the floor from making noise.

He began to drop the thickened pine-slime there. As much as he wanted to save Fred, a deepening hatred for Howard grew with each shortening breath.

Partly, he hoped to stumble upon Howie beforehand so he could break the little fucker's neck and kill him first.

A strange hoot echoed in the stairwell.

Something about the sound made his temples flare with pain. Where had he heard it before?

Thinking about the short sound sent his stomach for a tumble. Pine gunk rolled up his throat and spewed through the half of his throat he could still use.

He retched five times before his stomach came close to settling. Terrance had hurled, but his equilibrium was solid.

It clicked.

The hoot belonged to the Sixth Street Gang. They called it their *hunting howl*.

Unless he could find Fred first, they were going to kill his friend–and anyone else they found on their turf.

Terrance loosened up. He kept his steps light but gave up a bit on silence to move quicker across the seventeenth floor.

"What the fuck is this shit?"

Terrence turned.

In a doorway, Fred's mohawked form bent and pulled at his leg. "Surrender." The quick code word for: *don't shoot me; we're too close and it'll hurt like a motherfucker.* He kept his Splatmaster pointed at the ground and continued trying to lift his leg. "I'm stuck in something."

"Easy, Leonardo."

Fred raised his gun. "How do you know that name?"

"Listen." Terrance spoke slowly so his slushy words could possibly be understood. "You guys need to call it a night." He pointed. "The Sixth Street Gang is coming up the stairs."

"What?" Fred's eyes went wide. He set his paintball gun down and started to untie his mid-calf Doc Martens.

"Also, don't trust Donatello and never do him any favors."

"What?" He continued working his laces. "Why?"

A faint hunting howl echoed into the hallway.

"Just don't." He moved back down to the stairwell. Terrance focused on remembering what Fred had told him. "*The bum* will be right…"

Fred called, "What about Rafael?"

"Don't worry about him." Terrance spat the sap on the door latch. "He's just an asshole." He hoped Fred would get the Denis Leary reference. They used to sing the song all the time.

He closed the door behind him and dug his hand into his throat. Two wiggles, and he spewed.

Terrance aimed, landing multiple volleys on the handle and door. He spread it in the crack with his other hand.

Wanting to cover the stairs, he jammed his fingers back in. His middle finger went above his tongue, but his index hit his throat.

The gunk traveled up his esophagus and onto his stuck middle finger. The sap rolled down his arm and filled his mouth.

As Howard probably intended, Terrance was suffocating on it.

Hoping to make an obstacle of his body, Terrance began down the stairs but blacked out before he hit the first turn.

+ + +

Terrance stood with several other Directors and the Human Resources Manager at the new time clock, which incorporated a fingerprint scan into attendance. He continued his passive resistance. "I simply don't like this kind of biometric scanner for clocking in."

"Would you prefer retina scanners?"

"No." He smiled at her. Such a smartass. "What if someone is looking for me and this fingerprint is how they find me?"

"Relax. This won't be connected to Skynet and…" She chuckled and presented the small square pad to get him on file. "…you are only in the system to enroll your employees."

"Okay." Terrance placed his finger on the scanner. "But know I'm only doing this because of your apropos eighties reference."

Enrolled, Terrance cut across the public area at work and started thinking back to his youth and how he had friends who he would have done anything for. They called themselves the three turtles.

"The bum was right."

His temples stung. Why were Fred's final words echoing from the past?

"Don't trust Donatello and never do him any favors."

Déjà vu washed over him. Terrance froze.

Howard would be coming around the corner.

Terrance averted his eyes, pulled his phone, and placed it to his ear to fake a conversation. "I've been listening to you rattle for five minutes, Eugene. Now it's your turn to listen to me. No way am I–"

A person drew close and wheezed, "Raph?"

Howard's syllable carried smoke. Terrance waved his hand to bat the smell away and moved around him. "–going to let that go for under two hundred and you know–"

"Terry?"

"–that it's a steal at that price." Refusing to look back, Terrance continued to his department.

THE WEIGHT OF SCALES

In a world where divine abilities only manifest in women after the age of fifty, magic marks wisdom.

Once the powers become apparent, a budding caster leaves behind her earthly ties to join a sisterhood where she learns how to serve the greater good.

Fifteen, and fresh from the five-year training period in the convent, Andrew heeds his first charge - investigate the raids around his birth city.

One

THE DOUBLE-PAN SCALE DANGLING FROM ANDREW'S left ear shifted before the one in his right. He slowed his pace and cast his gaze about to find the source behind the registration. Squat blackberry bushes exuding the smell of home grew twenty feet away on both sides of the long, wide road leading to Shellyberg.

Before *being called*, he would hide in those bushes to sling berries at wagons heading to Port Cassandra.

Patient, he would lay in wait long enough for crickets to resume their chirping, not tipping his hand to astute wagon drivers.

Whoever was here did not know that subtlety or rushed to ambush.

Using his teachings to hold an emotionless face, Andrew's mouth watered at the opportunity to use his abilities. Since both earrings had shifted, The Laws of Balance allowed for him to react, in kind, to what may have been planned for him.

He rose to his toes and swayed at the hips. The air around him responded, making him the eye of the gusts encircling him. Rolling his shoulders, he fanned his arms at the surrounding bushes, massaging them.

Yelps rose from the writing bushes as thorns, minded when finding a hiding place, moved with the motions of Andrew's hands. He rolled his wrist toward his chest, and several loose blackberries flew to him and floated in the swirling wind for an afternoon snack. "Oh." Andrew plucked a berry from the air into his mouth. The flavor of his youth exploded and a fond sigh escaped as he chewed. As though he had not known, he continued, "Is there someone in the bushes?"

"Now!" Four bodies rose, each with both hands full of berries. Without care for what may result, eight fistfuls of blackberries were launched.

Andrew dropped his left heel near the ground and spun. The berries intended to stain his flowing white frock joined the ones he had pulled in, orbiting around him. Their action exposed, he could do equal to them. Andrew toyed with the idea of flinging some of the blackberries back.

The Rule of Purpose, the second of his three tenets, guided him toward the higher road. Andrew cupped his hands and dropped his heels to the ground. The spinning wind slowed, filling his hands to capacity with berries before returning to a near standstill, dropping the excess to the earth.

He had passed his tenth name day before *The Radiance* shown through him. Andrew had been part of the Berry Boys–a group of rascals whose worst crime was dotting passing merchants when the wind took their tasty, and plentiful, munitions.

Andrew scanned the faces as he brought a berry to his nose and inhaled the bouquet before placing it in his mouth. The four in faded town guard leather armor and high boots remained in the bushes around him. Though their features were stretched from five years of growth, Andrew became certain he was standing amongst old friends. He turned and met each's eyes as he recalled, "Binion. Geoff. Lange." Andrew paused at the last one. Instead of elongating from growth, the last boy's face had widened to resemble his childhood nickname. "Toad?"

The name brought a dagger to Toad's hand. "I go by Bull." His voice had deepened beyond norm and his words came out in bass-filled croaks. Given his massive size, Andrew could see why he had a new nickname, but it was hard not to keep thinking of him by his old moniker.

Geoff cleared his throat, trying to lower it to sound more demanding. "How do you know us, Lady?"

Lange rubbed his hands. His eyes passed over Andrew's frock as though he could see through. "I'll like to know *her.*"

Binion placed his hand on the pommel of his shortsword and rattled it against the scabbard. "Yes, how *do* you know us?"

All of their voices had dropped, while Andrew's had retained its prepubescent androgynous pitch. "Clean your mind." He advised Lange. "You won't like what you find here." Hands on his hips, Andrew faced their ringleader. "Binion, it's me, Drew."

Binion's face was blank.

Andrew looked to the others. Lange's lips worked side to side as though he was trying to mentally navigate a maze. Since the blond was not looking at his face, Andrew turned back to Binion.

Toad put his dagger away and rasped, "I thought only old women could use magic."

Choosing to be chivalrous, Lange chastised Toad, "Show some respect." He began to edge through the bushes to the road. "Please forgive my boneheaded friend, My Lady. The Sisterhood doesn't travel this way that often." As though a curious afterthought, Lange absently stroked his scabbard and asked, "Is it true about the Virtuous Vows?"

"Steve. Stop." Andrew unsuccessfully tried to balance his two handful of berries into a pile in one hand before he pulled his hair together behind him. "Does the name Andrew Seamstress ring a bell?"

"Holy shit." A pop came from Geoff, who clamped his hands over his slacked jaw. "Sorry. I mean, uh, crap." Geoff squinted as he stared, trying to pierce the fog of time. "Is that really you, Dirty Drew?"

Andrew rolled his eyes and gave his childhood response. "Yes, in the flesh."

"Why," Geoff started as he and the others began to close the distance between them, "why do you have long hair?"

Andrew glanced at the discarded berries around his feet, wishing he could change the waste like he could change the answer. "Tradition."

Toad questioned, "Why are you wearing earrings?"

"They are not simple ornaments." His defensive tone registered on their faces, and he realized he had not answered the question.

Andrew placed another berry into his mouth, squished it against the roof of his mouth, and, taking a moment to regain his composure, rolled the air from his mouth up to his nose. Shellyberg truly did have the best berries in the southern realm. "They represent my graduation from in The Insolate Sisterhood and enable me to act in accordance with my office."

Lange's eyes were no longer traveling up and down Andrew's torso but were fixed on his crotch as disgust weighed on the corners of his mouth. "Why are you wearing a dress?"

"This is tradition and function." Andrew fought the urge to flourish the full-length garment as was common when discussing the reasoning. "Much of our magic is based upon being able to move. Anything that restricts our movement also restricts our magic." He sighed. "I must beg your trust in knowing that this is better than the alternative."

Binion finally spoke again and questioned, "Same for the bare feet?"

Andrew checked to make sure his feet were showing. His leather hem, the only part of his frock not spun from cotton, hung to the ground. Recalling the spin, Andrew nodded.

The ringleader crossed his arms and tilted his head back in consideration. "So, what do we call you, then?"

Having asked the question of many of his Sisters, Andrew had the answer memorized. "Least to say, I am not older, so *Grandmother* will not fit. Nor am I female, so *Sister* would be equally out of place. Old terms, both *Radiant* and *Destined*, would work to denote my place in society and in service under The Good Lady's grace."

As though Andrew had not spoken, Binion offered through a smile, "How about Anne? It has a dash of your new life and a touch of your real name."

Andrew's head shook hard against the idea. The scales dangling from his earlobes slapped against his cheeks and neck. Before he could verbalize how much he did not want the nickname, Toad pointed his wide finger at Andrew's earrings and trailed it down through the air to the hem before asking the question that had plagued Andrew's thoughts on his way south. "Anne, how do you think your father's going to take this?"

Two

Often doubling as premium market space, Shellyberg's Great Hall faintly smelled of fish but was vacant of merchants. Outside, the surrounding ground fared slightly better, but Andrew knew all of the faces–locals, vendors, and patrons alike. The ever-present amber and orange streamers of his youth, colors showing fealty to Duchess Buckmore, were absent. The bare sconces and standard holders set high near the ceiling whispered of secession.

Andrew covertly chewed the last of the blackberries as his childhood friends escorted him to the center of the hall. The four came to a stop and Andrew cut his step short to not walk into them.

Binion raised his chin to project his voice to the far end. The scale on Andrew's left ear shifted forward, warning him of Binion's tomfoolery before the introduction echoed through the hall. "Lord Flower, The Sisterhood has heard of our plight and have sent Grandmother Anne to assist in sorting things out."

Andrew wanted to slap Binion upside the head.

If things had not changed, nicknames given by Binion tended to stick. His scale in his right ear shifted forward. The results of the action would be favorable.

Lord Flower sat in the former Governess's high-backed chair. A dozen guards, in newly dyed deep-and-light-blue-studded leather armor, stood idle near the similarly clad lord, the only visible difference between them being that Flower's face was not hidden behind a dropped visor. Like Binion, the Lord lifted his chin. "Tell the *good* Sister that we have this situation under control. Tell her we appreciate the care, but the rule of woman has failed us." He adjusted a gaudy ruby amulet to be over the center of his chest and settled into the seat. "Tell her we are doing what men must and what only men can."

An old, common saying flitted through Andrew's mind. When he had first stepped into their holy grounds, he overheard his Sisters whisper *Men are made for war.* After he mastered his first dance, only the most obstinate Sisters continued saying it when they thought he was not around.

Two hundred feet away, Andrew's scales could not weigh the purpose or possible results of the Lord's words. His feet tightened. The cold from the stones beneath his bare feet was considerably warmer than the reception thus far. Refused casual conversation distance, Andrew spoke as though it had been granted–his volume woefully low for the large room. "Thank you for your greeting, Lord. If you would but share your plight, I might be able to grant insight."

Lord Flower leaned on the right arm of the chair to look at him as he spoke. Once, Andrew was the tallest among his friends, now he was a head shorter, as though they'd had an additional two years to grow. The Lord raised his chin. "I see her lips move, but cannot hear her words."

"Lord." Toad's voice rolled across the hall, the deep garble dying on the walls. "A lady does not yell."

The guard to the Lord's right yelled, "Maybe they should."

When the laughter died down, Binion repeated Andrew's response with the same volume he used for the introduction.

Lord Flower stood, pointing toward the door. "Tell her she may have two loaves of bread and the pick of our berries, but her help is refused." He set his hand on the hilt of his longsword. "Jamestown will resolve this with steel."

Andrew narrowed his eyes at the thinly veiled threat and focused on the Lord's face. He whispered, "Guys, is that James Flower? The old Jailor?"

Having been caught the most for their past shenanigans, Geoff nodded.

He returned to speaking in normal tones. "I appreciate the berries and I'll gladly accept bread heels, but please know, Lord Flower, I'll do as The Good Lady wills." Andrew curtsied as Binion relayed his rhyme.

"Enjoy my city and may the morning sun find you walking north." The Lord gave a shallow bow and a dismissive wave.

Flinging his hair, Andrew spun and walked. His friends shuffled behind; Toad passed to open the door for him. Applicative, Andrew touched the sides of his dress and bent at the neck and knees before he stepped out into the open square.

A soft breeze carried the salt from the ocean, and distant gulls hovered on the wind. Port Cassandra appeared much closer to Shellyberg than Andrew remembered. There was a colossal five-mast ship docked on the rolling azure waves and, unloading cannons, the crew sung a chorus of *heaves* and *hos*.

His friends filed out as Andrew turned his gaze to the northern forest. Thicker than he recalled, it remained cleared away from the main road but had overtaken the narrower roads to Carolberg to the north-west and Michelletown to the north-east. Had the Lord let the growth happen to place a nature-based embargo on both cities?

Andrew scanned the vendors and patrons–all men. Lowering his voice to a whispered, "Can't believe he named the city after himself." The men eyed his dress. "Where are the women?"

Toad groaned. "Sent away."

Before the door closed, the Lord called. "John's Son."

Though the few patrons and vendors turned in their direction, none came forward.

Andrew faced his friends and, about to voice a question, he discovered three of his friends' foreheads were raised in surprise or confusion at Lange.

Steve sheepishly turned back. "I'll catch up." Opening the door an inch wider than his body, he slipped in, and the door closed.

It may have been obvious, but Andrew verified, "I take it that Lange being called *John's Son* does not happen often?"

Though Geoff and Toad's surprise eased, Binion blinked at the door. His mouth worked small, soundless circles.

"It's a right of passage." Geoff shrugged as though it did not bother him, but his lowered eyelids and knotted brow spoke otherwise. "A man of the guard takes you under his wing and you shed your mother's name."

"Yup," Toad agreed. Andrew half-expected his friend's neck and torso to pillow from the one deep syllable. "He'll be a Blue Stud before the end of the month."

His fists in tight balls, Binion spoke while he faced the door. "It has to do with the jail."

Not sure if the deposed childhood leader was speaking to them, Andrew offered, "We should investigate it."

"Damn right." Singled-minded, Binion turned and apologized to the form in white. "So sorry, Grandmother." His fist opened and he shook in place when he registered Andrew's face. Binion's cheeks deepened as he bit his lip at his–more awkward than the first–slip.

Speaking in a heightened pitch, Andrew gave a small curtsey and a wide smile. "Forgiven."

Binion's bottom lip disappeared into his mouth. "Man…"

Having spent a few days in there before, Andrew headed toward Port Cassandra's jail. He waved his arm to beckon his friends. "Come on."

THREE

CONSTRUCTED FROM IMPORTED BLACK BRICK, THE squat prison sat far away from the other dock buildings on the far west end of the pier, like a mole on the otherwise undeveloped beachfront's skin. Though the crew halted their heave-ho chorus to stare at Andrew as he, Binion, Geoff, and Toad turned to go down the pier, the seagulls continued their insistent calls.

The first few months within the high-walled convent, roughly in the middle of the Jennings Plains, were torture. The air only smelled of grass and mint. This close to the waters he had grown up around, Andrew inhaled deeply as the wood underfoot worked to remove the sand on his soles. The corners of his mouth rose when the fondly remembered salty taste registered.

"Welcome back." Next to him, Binion offered the greeting Andrew thought he would have heard on the road.

Though not guarded, every possible entry into the jail was locked. Each of the Berry Boys had snuck in to take a sweet treat to a captured friend, but the few windows, which used to have play, were barred with a diagonal slat. The main floor of cells was empty and the thick layers of dust inside marked the jail as being years out of use or service.

Andrew chuckled. The sight would drive Sister Fairweather into a mad cleaning frenzy.

They were out of sight at the least public of the dark oaken doors.

The ship's crew returned to chanting their work.

Andrew focused on his scales as he considered forcing his way in. His left leaned forward. According the Rule of Purpose, he was in the right. However, the rear cup on his right was rocked back further on the fulcrum than he had previously experienced. It felt as though real weight had been placed on it. According to the Mark of Action, the results of going through with what he had in mind outweighed his intention.

The Laws of Balance bound his hands. Though well intended, the outcome for breaking in would outstrip his want to act honorably. Dismayed, Andrew stepped away.

His left scale returned to a perfect balance, but the burden on his right ear increased. Wincing, he leaned his head. Decision made, his left scale rocked forward again and the load on his right ear eased as he began to move in place.

Praying that what he willed was in line with what The Good Lady would want, he moved his hips in a circle and allowed the exaggerated movement to roll his shoulders for counterbalance.

The gale winds whipped around him. His friends backed away, shielding their eyes from captured debris and denoting the shape and speed of the focused whirlwind. Andrew spun a tight circle and focused every generated knot at the door.

Split vertically, the two halves of door smashed inward. One half flew ten feet into the rear storage room. Still held by the lower hinge, the other half leaned diagonally away from the entrance.

Binion stepped to the entrance and gave a wry grin. "I don't suppose you have a flint box somewhere in that dress?"

Andrew returned the face and rolled his eyes. He moved out of the shadow and raised his hands above his shoulders. Swaying side to side with his fingers wide apart, Andrew rolled his wrists toward his face. "Sweet Sun," Andrew addressed the distant orb as a revered elder. "Please lend me your grace." As though lit from within, the scales began to light.

Geoff reached to touch when Andrew stepped back to the building and the shadows angled away from him. "Are they hot?"

Andrew batted his hand away. "No."

Toad lumbered forward. "I'll take point." Binion and Geoff moved to form a line behind Andrew.

"We know the first floor is empty." Andrew placed a hand on Toad's shoulder. "Best head to the basement and cellar cells."

Toad batted Andrew's hand away. "You touch like a girl."

Binion and Geoff erupted into surprised laughter.

Andrew shook his hand and silenced them with a shaming glance. "Sorry about that."

"It's okay."

Dust motes meandered in the residual current, separating and occasionally chasing each other as they swirled like fish in the ocean. Being careful of splinters, Andrew stepped in behind Toad. The air held a slight whiff of stale urine, and the floating neglect collected on his tongue.

Toad moved from the storage area, through the kitchen, and paused in the main room. From behind, Toad did not appear to have a neck and his head swiveled on his shoulders between the three possible directions.

Andrew remembered the one ahead led to the Jailor's office and the entrance, but could not recall which led to his quarters or to the two sublevels of additional cells.

From the rear, Geoff reminded, "Left."

Toad nodded and clumped as directed. He made the obvious right and stopped at the second door on the right. They entered the small room and began to move stacked tables and chairs in search for the cellar door.

When they found it, it held the slightest trace of dust caused by their stirring, with a large pile near the hinges where it folded over.

Toad clambered down the stairs. Without ambient light from the windows, Andrew's earrings threw harsh shadows down the jail cell corridor.

Silence swallowed all outside noise, and the heavy steps of his friends were the only noise in the still.

The acidic stench of recent urine assaulted his nose. Andrew moved close on Toad's side to allow his right scale to shine as straight as possible. About to grab Toad's shoulder, Andrew pulled his hand back. "Hold. Go back."

Geoff called from the back. "What? Why?"

Andrew squeezed to get past Binion. "The smell lessened."

"It did?" Geoff asked. Now at the head of the party, he started back toward the stairs.

Searching where his scales lit the fleeting shadows, Andrew came to a stop in front of a cell where the shadows did not go as deep into the privy bin. "Here."

The other three squeezed in to see the form in the shadows under the bed move. Only the glint across deep purple eyes showed something inside was staring back at them.

Andrew's left earring rocked on full tilt. It had the worst of intentions.

Toad grumbled, "What is it?" His angle did not allow for a clear view. When no one answered, he croaked, "Guys?"

Four

The stench of filth became stronger when the form moved away from the wall. Trying to drive the awful taste of the air away, Andrew's tongue watered, to no avail–he did not dare to swallow.

A length of chain scraped against the floor when slender black fingers grabbed the bottom bunk.

Andrew's toes tightened and gripped the stone floor when the pitch, buxom female came into full view. Clinging to what modesty she was afforded, the woman had the itchy grey blanket pulled together under her arms. It fell to just above her knees.

"Wow." Geoff thumped Andrew's arm and pointed to what they both could see. "What is she?"

The sisters often sung songs about the old creatures of the world, but none had been seen in the last four hundred years. The first stanza of the eldest lyrics from those days described how the most plentiful of monstrous races, orcs and goblins, disappeared overnight.

Toad shoved to see, and the rest stumbled sideways.

Geoff lost his footing and thumped to the ground. Andrew grabbed the bars to keep from going over. Binion fell past him and was sprawled next to Geoff, their legs entangled as they both tried to stand at the same time.

"My, aren't you a big one?" she cooed, her hand loosening on the blanket. "And so innocent."

Andrew tried to push Toad and failed.

However, Toad recoiled from his touch and hopped back to where he had been.

Binion and Geoff untangled and stood. Andrew pushed them, and they moved. "Stay out of sight, guys."

In unison, they asked, "Why?"

"It's a night hag."

"They have nothing to fear from me." The hag shook her shapely leg, exposing more dark skin, and the chain cuffed to her ankle shone with the same radiance as Andrew's earrings but turned mundane grey in the shadows. "I'm tethered."

Feeling a building heat in his crotch, Andrew stepped beyond the cell to be out of view of the temptress.

Toad peaked into the cell.

Both Binion and Geoff tugged on his thick shoulder to pull him back. "What are we going to do?"

"Give me a minute." Hip kicked out to the side, Andrew placed his hands on his waist. His head leaned to the side as he started to recite the songs in his head.

Toad took a step further away. "He stands like a girl, too."

Andrew recalled over sixty songs having to do with demons or witches. While some mentioned facing the infernal creatures, the songs all ended vaguely with the heroine–usually of The Sisterhood–being victorious.

"Guys?" Lange's voice came from the cellar door. "Are you down there?"

"Yup." Toad answered.

Binion punched him.

Geoff punched him.

In returned, the lummox frowned. "What?"

Andrew sighed.

"It's not safe to be down there." A set of footsteps started down the stairs. "I've heard rumors of-" Stepping into the hallway, Lange paused, his eyes locked on the glowing scales. "Anne, just so you know, that's sharper than the floating berries trick you did earlier."

"Come on over," Toad rumbled. "You ain't seen nothing yet."

Lange drew closer. "What are you talking about?"

"I know that voice," The hag murmured. "Are you finally here for a go to earn your studs, or would you simply prefer another show?"

Andrew locked eyes with Lange. "You knew she was here?"

"No."

His left scale teetered forward while his right went back. Andrew's eyes narrowed. Lange lied with good intentions, but the outcome was out of balance with the untruth. Andrew flipped a palm up and motioned for more information. "Is there anything else you would like to add?"

Lange opened his mouth.

Both of Andrew's scales tilted back.

Lange's eyes shifted to the shadows.

Though he had not said a word, Andrew understood.

Lange's eyes widened, he pivoted, and ran back to the stairs.

Andrew's bare feet slapped on the stone as he gave chase. He called, "After him!"

Boots clumped behind him. His friends were on his tail.

Andrew turned the corner into the kitchen to see Lange duck under the plank at the rear door. The flash of the blond set both of his earrings rocking back.

Geoff called, "Bull?"

Andrew spun. Binion was right behind him, but Toad was not in sight. He considered going back. His left scale shifted forward for his intentions, but the right continued to slowly tilt toward the backside. He measured leaving Toad to catch Lange. His left earring shot backward, yanking Andrew's head as the right sustained its measured decline.

"I'll get him." Andrew slipped between them. "Try to stop Lange before he can alert the others." With a hope to be heard over the growing distance, he raised his voice as he turned corners to get back to the cellar door. "Be careful!"

The privy stench came back when his feet left the wood and slapped on to the stone at the bottom.

Toad stood outside the cell with his hand on the latch. The corner of his wide mouth obscenely stretched upward as his eyes were fixed on whatever the hag was doing to keep him entranced. The thick end of a baleful plum tentacle of light writhed in the air an inch outside the cell. Answering the call, white light began to dance from Toad's eyes toward the purple.

Eyes closed tight, Andrew ran and leapt onto Toad's side, clambered onto his back, and covered his eyes. Perfect warmth bathed his palms and what was beyond the back of his hands slipped through his fingers and into Toad.

Unfrozen, Andrew felt Toad's weight transfer back, and he tensed at what was coming.

His big friend stumbled back, inadvertently slamming him into the cell bars behind them. The slap of pain sprung Andrew's arms open. Toad stumbled to the side.

On his back, Andrew rolled onto his hands and knees. His dress had come up to his backside and the excess made trying to crawl forward in the frock futile.

The hag tried to grab his attention. "Look here, boy. Bet your Sisters never showed you this."

Her sultry voice conjured a vision of her dark legs spread wide to the unknown in Andrew's head. He felt a twitch in his manhood bound under him but refused to look. Andrew extended his knees and somersaulted to relative safety.

Toad jogged down the hall, looking back past Andrew to make sure they were not being chased.

Andrew did not dare to look.

A wind chased them up the stairs, out the back, and into the sunlight. Protected by the sun's grace, Andrew looked back when the door slammed behind him.

The split showed where it had been cracked, but the door was back in place, keeping the darkness secured inside.

Andrew spun and threw his fist into the air. "Thank you for your grace, Good Lady."

About to perform a short dance of gratitude to his Goddess, Andrew turned when dread dropped Toad's deep voice an octave. "Anne."

Andrew glanced to where his thick finger pointed.

Binion and Geoff were running back toward them with dozens of blue-studded leathered guards giving chase.

FIVE

THE ROLLING WAVES LAPPED A HAPHAZARD BEAT
against the beach, and the ship's crew heaved with the
rush and hoed with the recede. Seagulls' cries wove
high pitches into the low sounds. Andrew wiggled his
toes on the beach before he dug in. A gentle wind rolled
scents from the road against the wind coming from the
ocean. Both gusts met at his center, kicking up the fine
sand. He opened his mouth to take in the mix of salt
and blackberries. Granules rose on the wind and into
his mouth. Andrew rubbed them against his palate. He
was home.

Just as deep waves threatened to drag the unseaworthy
to its briny depths, the coming crush of Flower's men in
blue-studded leather promised to take his life and the lives
of his friends if he did not properly captain them.

"Come on." Andrew started running the length of the
pier, Toad's steady, heavy thumps slowly falling behind.
He waved one hand above him to get Binion and Geoff's
attention. Directing them, he pointed to where the five-
mast ship was being unloaded.

They adjusted their slant.

Andrew looked past his friends. Another rank of blue spilled from Shellyberg. These did not give chase. Instead, they aimed their bows toward the clouds. Andrew still worked to get to the location he had set and waited until they loosed their arrows to stop and spin.

He drew a circle in the sand with one toe as he rolled his torso and spun his hand in the air. His earrings swung with his momentum, their potential guidance momentarily lost as the arrows began their fall.

Malice in his heart, Andrew dug his toes out to drop to his knees. He slapped the sand with both hands.

The arrows' descent sharpened. Rocking, his scales attempted to balance; left forward, right back, signaling the outcome before they came down.

He heard pain-filled cries and looked up to see the damage. The volley of arrows dropped on the men chasing his friends, thinning the number of pursuers. Arrow tips dug where he wanted them to and the weight of his right ear, marking the results of his action as bad, confused him.

The only man in blue with his visor up, Lord Flower, astride a pure white steed, charged from the great hall. The hooves were smoke and sent tremors through the earth as the horse galloped with unearthly speed to close the gap between its rider and his men.

Andrew popped back to his feet. Toad moved past him on the pier and neared the rally point where Binion and Geoff stood with their shortswords drawn.

The ship's crew stopped working again. Those who were dockside gathered a distance from his friends.

Andrew yelled to the seamen as he ran, "How many of you remember Port Cassandra and Shellyberg?"

Used to only answering to their Captain's call, none of the men raised their hands, but Andrew found some nods.

Binion called, "Arrows!"

Swinging his hips, Andrew lifted his arms to the sky from his chest and arched his hands outward. His earrings swung forward. The stream of arrows parted in the middle, flying wide on either side of the advancing footmen.

"The man on horseback has killed the trade here and plans war for Duchess Buckmore."

A man in a wide-brimmed hat called from the bow, "What do we care for any land rule?"

Andrew checked the distance. The footmen were closing, and Lord Flower was nearly in line with the coming crush. "Does her gold not spend?" The archers abandoned their bows and started to make their way to the beach. He looked to the captain. "Do you believe a dance of an Insolate Sister, depicting your bravery here, would fail to move the Duchess to pay you for your merit?"

Toad bowled Andrew over, and he slid across the sand. "Anne, watch out!"

Prone, Andrew scanned for what Toad warned him of and found four black orbs before they dodged around Toad. His large friend's attempt to knock Andrew from the path was for naught, as each orb beat into his abdomen.

Andrew rolled to his back, rocked his legs toward his chest, and kicked his legs up while pushing off the sand. His bare feet landed on the pier. He rose onto his tiptoes and swung his shoulders counter to his hips. The pain in his abdomen lanced with each gyration as the thunderous hooves closed.

He kicked his leg out and brought his heel in for rapid revolutions. Splinters dug into his toes as sand rose into a sudden, savage twister. In the eye, Andrew let the full force fly at the lord.

The fury hit Flower like a lance and dehorsed him. Without his rider, the horse became wisps of smoke and faded. The driving wind knocked the amulet from the lord, and when the sand clouds thinned, an emaciated corpse rose from where the man had fallen.

Not believing what had been the jailor, Andrew's mouth gaped slightly. "A lich?"

Clad in tattered, rich purple robes adorned with a crimson skull over a slash of black lighting, the lich patted its chest and then scanned around it.

Andrew spotted the ruby amulet, no less gaudy without illusion. Between his battered abdomen and splintered feet, he could not summon a gust strong enough to keep the item beyond the lich's undead grasp.

"Aim!" Andrew's gaze found the captain, his cutlass extended. He sliced his blade through the air. "Fire!"

Dockside, cannons roared.

The balls were at their mark before Andrew could turn his head. Clouds of sand were sent high into the sky.

"Ready!"

A team of three seamen worked the cannon with black power, tamped it, and loaded the ball in five seconds.

"Sister." Andrew looked to the captain, who remained focused on where the lich had been. "You best dance lighting for the Duchess."

The sand settled on a ruby amulet, but the undead was gone.

Amulet in hand, Andrew walked among those he thought he had injured. Gratefully, most of the arrows had sliced through clothes, dragging the footmen down with their force. There was only one injured, with an arrow through his leg, and one dead.

Three shafts, fletching deep, protruded from the top of Lange's skull.

A bitter taste rose into his mouth. Andrew spat. The fulcrum of his right earring, the Mark of his Actions, tilted back slightly and would not recover.

Andrew turned his gaze to the one man injured by the arrow. Others had already broken the shaft, pulled it through, and bound his wound.

Letting his sorrow fill his chest, Andrew raised his hands to the sky and brought himself low to the ground. He had let darkness overtake him, and he silently prayed to The Good Lady for a sign of forgiveness.

He held the position.

"Thank you, Sister." Framed by the sun, the injured man stood above him, holding the bloody bandage; the wound had closed.

Andrew shielded his eyes and looked into his father's smiling face.

TREAT ME

Extra

DAY

Blondie lifted her head and looked toward the kitchen. A ruffling, similar to Little Alpha digging at the bottom of his box for a toy hidden among the bland-tasting plastic blocks, caught her ear.

Listening for the telltale secondary sound, her ears rose to allow space between her floppy ears and golden facial fur. She was motionless, waiting. The sharp puncture, a signal she was going to get moist food mixed in with her standard fare, set her legs into motion.

There was always a meaty treat first.

Coming from the den, she paused for a moment. Alpha Female moved side-to-side, waving the small white square, which looked like a bone. By swinging it, Alpha Female was making noise across the room.

Blondie had tasted the non-bone on multiple occasions and discovered it was as flavorless as other plastic things. It was only after she had solved the challenge and worked the seams did she discover it did not have marrow at the center.

After that, but before she got her mouth on the other similar object, Blondie noticed it had an annoyingly bitter smell. Though rare, she went against what her nose warned her away from and found the new taste was the worst.

She padded around Alpha Female to the kitchen where Alpha Male waited for her. Her tail wagged for a moment and she sniffed at where the wooden floor became tile. There was a faint scent, grape. Her eyes followed her nose and spied the thin flavor sticks Little Alpha leaves behind after getting rid of the delicious ice-like coating.

She feared the day when Little Alpha would realize the best part of the Popsicle, the part he regularly casts aside, was at the center.

Blondie looked at Alpha Male, who was still observing her. Remembering dinner and what she had to do, she sat on her haunches and waited. Soon he would pull the top of the can away, mix it in her bowl, and walk it to the sliding door, which kept the Outside out. She licked her chops.

Alpha Male turned away, and she heard the short, crisp sound. The wet food was now exposed to the air on the counter. A long time ago, she put her front paws on the edge to see what was up there, but that was before she was not allowed on the tile.

He turned back and she glimpsed the thin but sharp-on-the-edges circular object which kept her food moist when he put it on the counter behind him.

Her gaze followed his hand, the wonderful treat-and-affection-giving thing. She licked her chops again. The wind maker on the ceiling pushed the enjoyable scent to her. It also stirred smells across the tile, and Blondie remembered the Popsicle stick.

Alpha Female squealed with delight, and Alpha Male left her food and treat on the counter to investigate.

Blondie turned her head but did not follow him. She was to be patient and wait. He would come back and, better than dinner food, she would receive a small, meaty treat.

Of all the things in the house she had managed to get her mouth on, the meaty treats tasted the best.

She licked her chops and waited.

Blondie yawned and lay still. He would come back.

She wanted to whimper for his attention, but whimpering never resulted in a meaty treat.

Lying there, the fan stirred air around the kitchen, bringing the grape Popsicle-stick smell. She sniffed around a bit and her nose directed her eyes to it again.

It was under the counter, but she was not allowed on the tile.

She stood and sniffed at the tile edge again before going to check on Alpha Male. He was resting on the couch—which held The Alphas' scents so well—and watching Alpha Female swing the non-bone.

Blondie went back to where the wood and tile met. She stared at the stick. The wooden goodness was about a neck length away.

Trying to figure a way to get to it without going on the tile, she paced.

Sidling next to the counter, she had figured out how.

Placing her font paws at the edge of the wood, Blondie licked her chops and stretched. She was a nose away. All she would have to do is extend her tongue and it was hers.

Night

Blondie sighed. Easing from her shame-curl, she set her muzzle on the inside edge of her cushion in the den. Though she slept there during most nights, few things were worse than being told *go to bed* when the rest of the pack was still up and active. They hadn't made their dinner, and hers sat on the counter.

She pressed her nose further into the cushion, sniffing. Following the whiff of chicken, a piece of dried food slid under her chin. Pulling back a bit, she fished it out, ate it, and went about searching for any other morsels she might have stashed away from dry food night. Nothing more.

She sighed again. Had she been in been in bed long enough? Alpha Male called her *bad girl* before sending her away. Her name wasn't bad girl, it was Blondie, but she knew. She knew it was The Alphas' way of telling her she had broken pack law.

The worst was hearing the snapping sound of her treat pouch sealing before Alpha Female closed it away behind doors. With paw and nose, Blondie used to be able to open them before Little Alpha started to grow and move on his own.

Blondie perked her ears and listened for Little Alpha. Though she would still be hungry, Little Alpha often petted her no mater what and, sometimes, they had been sent to bed together. Though they had done bad, lying next to Little Alpha on his bed made the punishment for breaking pack law bearable.

It must have been long enough. She remembered being driven away, but not why.

Thinking of Little Alpha, she slunk from her bed to where she could see into his territory. His cars and stuffed animals were on the floor, but he was not in his room.

Being careful, she poked her head into the area where the pack did most of their living. Alpha Male and Alpha Female were piled next to each other on the couch, staring at the sound box across the room. Head averted, eyes on the Alphas, Blondie took a step into the room, and then another.

Alpha Male spied her, and she froze. His eyebrows and lips drew tight, but he did not send her back to her room.

He must have forgotten, too.

Blondie slowly continued through the living territory, and her nails on the wooden floor never sounded louder.

Alpha Male's gaze followed, but he let her pass.

With a quick sideways glance into the tile area, she found the Popsicle stick missing. It was probably placed behind the door where the Alphas store food beneath the pack to take into Outside.

Near her bowl, Blondie sniffed at the peanut butter mixed with Little Alpha's scent. She quickly lapped at the cool water before following her nose to find Little Alpha. She owes it to him to clean his fingers and face so Alpha Female doesn't yell at him.

Blondie sniffed around the table where The Alphas eat and found crumbs dropped by Little Alpha. She licked them and then her chops. She continued on his trail, hoping to find more.

She paused at the flap in the door keeping the Outside out and turned a circle. Little Alpha's trail was strongest here, but he must have been on the other side.

He's not supposed to be Outside alone. She needed to get him before he got in trouble for breaking pack law again.

A quick glance back assured her that Alpha Male and Alpha Female were not following her.

To keep the flap from making sound, she eased her head through. Little Alpha's peanut butter scent is here, but there's different smells on the air.

Blondie scanned the area to see Little Alpha at the side gate. Though the bars there did not allow either of them to squeeze through, it was a good location to keep an eye on their territory and wait for The Alphas to return from hunting.

Little Alpha was looking toward the street. Had he spied the Moon already? The flap dragged across Blondie's back and tail as she exited to see.

Arms reached in. One hand took a hold of Little Alpha's clothes as his small hands struggled against the other covering his mouth.

Muscles along her side and hind legs drew tight before she tore across the backyard, eyes fixed on the arms lifting Little Alpha from the yard.

Blondie leapt and bit.

Her teeth sunk into the stranger's coat as her hind legs came back to the ground. She whipped her head and growled as her extra weight brought the arms down.

The hands dropped Little Alpha and slipped from the coat to run away.

Blondie barked after him. *Warning: Stay away from our territory, stay away from Little Alpha.*

Between her barks, she could hear Little Alpha crying. A fresh surge of anger rolled through her chest, and she barked harder.

The stranger went beyond view, but Blondie continued.

Alpha Male and Alpha Female arrived.

Alpha Female scooped up Little Alpha, and Alpha Male hopped the fence.

Blondie tried to push through the bars, but they always kept her in. Unable to hunt with Alpha Male, she shadowed Alpha Female inside; she held Little Alpha tight.

+

Alpha Male returned. He took time to check on Little Alpha and then went to the door hiding the meaty snacks.

Blondie followed.

"Good girl," he said.

Her tail began to wag.

Alpha Male opened the pouch and put his hand inside.

She sat on her haunches but could not stop her tail from wagging in anticipation.

About the Author:

Christopher Watson hales from Las Vegas and currently resides in southern Florida. Favoring fantasy, science fiction, and paranormal occult, he's written over a hundred short stories, a score of novellas, and half a dozen novels.

FORTHCOMING WORK:

SCIENCE FICTION
I Could've Been A Nobody
Prison Moon

FANTASY
Better Off Dead, Lightning Chuck 2
Dead Letters

ELSEWHERE
E
P
PUBLISHING

THANK YOU FOR READING.

For a complementary electronic version
of this physical work, please go to:
www.elsewherepublishing.com/shop

Load this collection into your cart
and enter the following code:
C0279P89G